MODERN HUMANITIES RESEARCH A
NEW TRANSLATIONS
VOLUME 8

FOUGERET DE MONBRON
(1706–1760)
MARGOT LA RAVAUDEUSE

TRANSLATED WITH AN INTRODUCTION AND NOTES BY
ÉDOUARD LANGILLE

Fougeret de Monbron (1706–1760)

Margot la ravaudeuse

Translated with an Introduction and Notes by
Édouard Langille

Modern Humanities Research Association
2015

Published by

The Modern Humanities Research Association,
Salisbury House
Station Road
Cambridge CB1 2LA
United Kingdom

First published 2015

ISBN 978-1-78188-189-7

www.translations.mhra.org.uk

Frontispiece by C. F. Fritzsch of the 1800 [1753] Hamburg (1st) edition

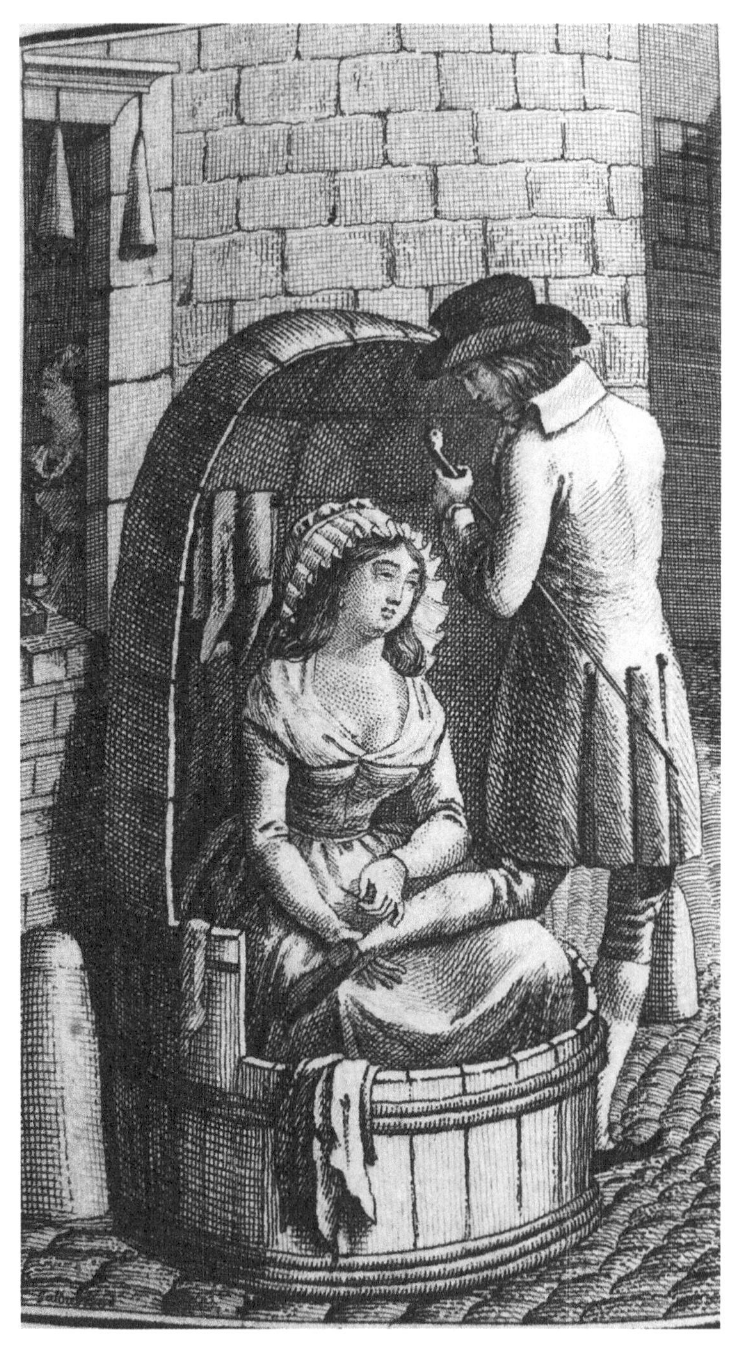

Frontispiece of the 1784 Paris edition (Lenoire)
'Before long, I was the best stocking darner in the neighbourhood'

CONTENTS

INTRODUCTION

Louis-Charles Fougeret de Monbron (1706–1760) was a minor French writer who shot like a meteor through the literary firmament of the 1740s and 1750s. Famous for his travels, his bizarre appearance, and his eccentric, antisocial personality, Monbron circled for a time in an outer orbit round Parisian literary life. He was a regular in the cafés and a familiar face at the *Comédie*, the *Opéra*, in the gaming houses, and in the *maisons closes*.[1] The young Diderot wrote of his hirsute brow and mad, jaundiced gaze, describing him memorably in his *Première Satyre* as 'l'homme au cœur velu' (the man with a ferocious heart).[2] Critics have suggested that this 'tiger on two legs' inspired the character of 'LUI' in Diderot's 'broken novel', *Le Neveu de Rameau*, written some time after 1761.[3]

Monbron was not only a colourful personality, he was also the author of a number of now largely forgotten works, including a tongue-in-cheek imitation of Voltaire's *Henriade*, entitled *La Henriade travestie* (1745).[4] Like other literary Frenchmen in the 1740s, Monbron was a zealous Anglophile. 'For me every Englishman was a divinity', he noted on the first page of his autobiographical essay *Le Cosmopolite, ou citoyen du monde* (1750), nowadays considered a significant source for Voltaire's *Candide* (1759).[5] True to his fervour for everything English, Monbron is credited with the first French translation of John Cleland's novel about prostitution, *Fanny Hill, Memoirs of a Woman of Pleasure* (1748), published in 1751 under the title *La Fille de Joye*.[6] We shall see presently that Cleland's novel played an important role in the genesis of Monbron's own novel on prostitution, *Margot la ravaudeuse* (or the *stocking darner*).

---

[1] Brothels.

[2] Literally: 'the man with the hairy heart'. Denis Diderot, 'Satire première', in *Œuvres complètes de Diderot*, ed. by H. Coulet (Paris: Hermann, 1989), XII, p. 14.

[3] Denis Diderot, *Le Neveu de Rameau*, critical edition with notes and lexicon compiled by Jean Fabre (Geneva: TLF, 1950), p. 113.

[4] Fougeret de Monbron, *La Henriade travestie en vers burlesques* (Berlin [Paris]: n. pub., 1745).

[5] 'Chaque Anglais étoit pour moi une divinité'. Fougeret de Monbron, *Le Cosmopolite, ou le citoyen du monde*, aux dépens de l'auteur (n.p. [Hamburg or London]: n. pub., 1750). For a modern critical edition see *Le Cosmopolite, ou le citoyen du monde*, ed. by Édouard Langille (London: MHRA, 2010), p. 1.

[6] Fougeret de Monbron, *La fille de joye. Ouvrage quintessencié de l'anglois* ([n.p.] Lampsaque: n. pub., 1751). For a modern edition see John Cleland, *Fanny Hill, la fille de joie*. Récit quintessencié de l'anglais par Fougeret de Monbron (Arles: Actes Sud, 1993). See also Dora Bienaimé Rigo, 'La prima versione francese di *Fanny Hill*', *Rivista di letterature moderne e comparate*, 34, Florence (1981), 249–70.

Although he was an Anglophile in the 1740s, Monbrons's enthusiasm for England turned sour a decade later. During the Seven Years' War, he penned an anti-English/anti-Voltaire pamphlet entitled *Le Préservatif contre l'Anglomanie* (1757).[7] Yet, despite his latter-day Anglophobia, Monbron was never fully reconciled to his homeland. True to his motto — *contemnere et contemni* (to despise and be despised) — his last work was an angry anti-Parisian pamphlet published in 1759. Interestingly, in *La Capitale des Gaules, ou la Nouvelle Babylone*, Monbron recognized his own caricature in the guise of *Candide*'s pessimistic philosopher, Martin.[8] Fougeret de Monbron died on 16 September 1760, aged fifty-four.

For a minor figure, Monbron's life is surprisingly well documented.[9] His father was a well-to-do government agent established in Péronne — the predicate *de Monbron* having been acquired early in the eighteenth century. Socially ambitious, in 1727 the elder Fougeret purchased a commission in the King's household guard for his youngest son. After just three years Louis-Charles resigned his commission under a cloud. Following this, Fougeret *père* attempted to rehabilitate the young man by securing for him the dignity of *valet de chambre ordinaire du roi* for 18 000 *livres*. The gilded gates of Versailles swung open to our former officer, who now could boast personal access to the King. Four years later, Monbron left Court because of his extreme moodiness.[10] Unsuited to life as a courtier, Monbron sold his position in the King's household and in 1738 took up residence in Paris. His later writings suggest that during these years he was no stranger to the dissipated life of the libertine, involving gaming, ladies of pleasure, and drunken Bacchanals. Rejecting his family's social ambitions, Monbron's aggressive brand of cynicism was consciously styled on that of the Ancient Greek philosopher Diogenes, the original 'cosmopolitan'. Without friends or social graces, Monbron was nevertheless determined to make his name in the republic of letters. In 1740, he published a libertine text, entitled *Le Canapé, couleur de feu*, based on Crébillon's *Le Sopha*.[11] The work was not well received.

Monbron's situation changed for the better in 1742 with the death of his father. In possession of a sizeable inheritance, he decided to emulate Voltaire and

---

[7] Fougeret de Monbron, *Le Préservatif contre l'Anglomanie* (Minorque [Paris]: n. pub., 1757).
[8] Fougeret de Monbron, *La Capitale des Gaules ou la Nouvelle Babilonne* (Bagdat [Paris]: Duchesne, 1759), 2e partie, p. 8. See É. Langille, 'La Place, Monbron et la genèse de *Candide*', in *Les 250 ans de* Candide, ed. by Nicholas Cronk and Nathalie Ferrand (Louvain-Paris-Walpole, MA: Peeters, 2014), pp. 337–46. See also Emmanuel Boussuge, 'Fougeret de Monbron à la Bastille et dans ses archives', *Revue d'histoire littéraire de la France*, 1 (2007), 157–66.
[9] Emmanuel Boussuge, *Situations de Fougeret de Monbron 1706–1760* (Paris: Champion, 2010).
[10] J. H. Broome, '*L'Homme au cœur velu*: the turbulent career of Fougeret de Monbron', *SVEC* 23 (1963), pp. 179–213.
[11] Fougeret de Monbron, *Le Canapé couleur de feu* (Amsterdam: Compagnie des libraires, 1714 [1741]).

journey to London. His first stay lasted only six weeks, and a second stopover in 1748 only eight. In the interim, Monbron taught himself enough English to translate and publish two works: Dodsley's *The Chronicle of the Kings of England*, and Thomas Corbett's *An Account of the Expedition of the British Fleet to Sicily, in the Years 1718, 1719 and 1720*.[12] In the meantime, his *Canapé, couleur de feu* was translated in 1742 and published in London under the title of *The Settee; Or Chevalier Commodo's Metamorphosis*.[13]

Having discovered the freedom of travel, Monbron indulged his wanderlust over a thirteen-year period by journeying throughout Europe, returning to Paris from time to time in order to replenish his finances. The English considered him a spy and his movements were monitored by the chancelleries of Europe. Back in France, he was twice incarcerated for his seditious writings, the first time from 7 November to 5 December 1748 in For-l'Évêque prison, and the second from 12 April to 25 September 1755 in the Bastille.

Le Cosmopolite, ou le citoyen du monde (1750) is Monbron's account of his travels during the War of the Austrian Succession (1740–1748): in England (1742, 1748), Constantinople (1742–1743), Italy (1745), Prussia (1745), Saxony (1746–1747), Spain (1747) and Portugal (1748). Widely read in its day, Monbron's sardonic narrative provided a template for other writers who imitated its world-weary tone. In English literature one can point to the work's influence on Goldsmith's *Citizen of the World* (1760) and *The Traveller* (1765), Smollett's *Travels through France and Italy* (1766), and Sterne's *Sentimental Journey* (1768). Sixty years after it was published, *Le Cosmopolite* fired the imagination of a poet of the first rank. The young Byron quoted its first paragraph on the title page of *Childe Harold's Pilgrimage* (1812).[14]

Le Cosmopolite is interesting for us because it provides an account of Monbron's arrest in the autumn of 1748, allegedly for penning *Margot la ravaudeuse*. 'My manuscriptwas shown to a triumvirate of scoundrels', he wrote in *Le Cosmopolite*'s concluding pages. 'These three lost no time accusing me in an anonymous letter to the Grand Inquisitor of the Police of having written a lampoon contrary to the interests of Church and State.'[15] The first page of the published novel returns to that incident and announces with characteristic sarcasm:

---

[12] *Chronique des rois d'Angleterre* écrite en anglais selon le style des anciens historiens juifs, par Nathan Ben Saadi, prêtre de la même nation; et traduite en français dans le même style (London: T. Cooper, 1743); *Histoire de l'expédition de l'amiral Byng dans la Sicile, en 1718, 1719 et 1720*, traduite de l'anglais par M.*** (London: Thomas Corbett, 1744).

[13] Fougeret de Monbron, *The Settee; Or Chevalier Commodo's Metamorphosis* (London: Samuel Harding, 1742).

[14] Byron, *Letters and Journals*, vol. 2, ed. Prothero (London: John Murray, 1898), pp. 39–40.

[15] 'Ce perfide [...] fut révélé mon secret à un triumvirat de coquins, qui m'accusèrent dans une lettre anonyme, adressée à l'inquisiteur de police, d'avoir composé un libelle contre la religion et le gouvernement.' *Le Cosmopolite, ou le citoyen du monde* (2010), p. 56.

> Here at last is Margot la ravaudeuse, a novel which General de la Pousse, encouraged by the corporation of harlots and their infamous henchmen, would have us believe constitutes a crime against the State. The author, accused of nothing less than having attempted to undermine the authority of religion, the government and the Sovereign, and fearing that his silence was in itself an admission of guilt, he had no choice but to publish the work, leaving the question of guilt or innocence entirely in the hands of the public.

At the time of his arrest in 1748, we can surmise that Monbron was in fact preparing *Margot* for publication. As suggested, he showed a manuscript entitled *Margot la ravaudeuse, ou la Tribade*, to his Grub Street cronies.[16] No sooner had he done so than he was denounced to the police by the clandestine bookseller Bonnin.[17] Upon arrest, his papers were seized, and the manuscript of his novel was presumably destroyed. We do not know whether more than one manuscript copy of *Margot* existed, but, once released from prison, Monbron must have partially rewritten the work; the published version of *Margot* contains no hint of *tribadisme*, or lesbian erotica. When it was finally brought out in Hamburg, it was with a false date (1800). Emmanuel Boussuge has recently shown that the novel most likely appeared in 1753, five years after it had been seized by the Parisian authorities.[18]

Like the diminutive 'Moll' in English (consider Defoe's Moll Flanders, or Moll Hackabout, the unfortunate prostitute portrayed in Hogarth's *A Harlot's Progress*, 1732), the name 'Margot' is suggestive of prostitution.[19] In the 1720s, *Margot la ravaudeuse* was the title of a vaudeville ditty, and it is likely that Monbron co-opted it from that source.[20] Another possible source might well be the 1739 prose comedy *Le Porteur d'Iau, ou les amours de la ravaudeuse* whose central character is a stocking darner named Margot.[21] The early editions of the novel show a young *Parisienne* darning socks in her barrel or tub, the customary stall of stocking menders in the eighteenth century.[22] Since publication, *Margot la ravaudeuse* has been reprinted in more than a dozen German, French and Belgian editions, twice under slightly modified titles: *Margot la ravaudeuse, histoire d'une prostituée*,[23]

---

[16] Boussuge, p. 163.

[17] Ibid., p. 252.

[18] Ibid., p. 282.

[19] See Villon's *Ballade de la grosse Margot*. See also John Farmer, *Vocabula Amatoria French / English Dictionary of Erotica* (n.p.: n. pub., 1896), p. 182; reprinted New York: University Books, 1966.

[20] Fougeret de Monbron, *Margot la ravaudeuse*, in *Romanciers libertins du XVIIIe siècle*, tome I, ed. by Patrick Wald Lasowski (Paris: Gallimard, Bibliothèque de la Pléiade, 2000), p. 1257.

[21] *Le Porteur d'Iau, ou les amours de la ravaudeuse*, in *Les Écosseuses ou les Œufs de Pâques* (Troyes: chez la veuve Oudot, 1739), pp. 9–61.

[22] The barrel is a reminder of Diogenes and his philosophy of cynicism.

[23] Fougeret de Monbron, *Margot la ravaudeuse, histoire d'une prostituée* (Hamburg: n. pub., 1774).

or *Margot la ravaudeuse, et ses aventures galantes*.[24] It was under this last designation that the work was translated into Italian in 1861: *Margot la conciacalze e le sue avventure galanti*.[25] After Monbron's death the novel appeared under two different titles hitherto unrecorded by literary historians concerned with the career of Fougeret de Monbron. In 1761 it was published in Amsterdam as *La Brunette ou Avantures d'une Demoiselle*.[26] Then, in 1796, it was reissued in London and Paris under yet another title: *Fanchette, danseuse de l'Opéra, histoire galante*.[27] *Margot* has been translated into Spanish (*Margot la remendona*), Dutch (*Margriet in de ton*), German (*Margot, die Flickschusterin*), Czech, and Serbian (*Margo krparka*). Surprisingly, given the book's notoriety, *Margot la ravaudeuse* was only once translated into English, in a 1967 dime-store edition. Following the lifting of America's restrictive laws on obscenity in 1966,[28] a publishing house in North Hollywood specializing in 'adult content' brought out a rough adaptation of the novel entitled *The Amorous Adventures of Margot*.[29]

It was not only in North America that racy novels had to be sold under the counter. For almost a hundred and fifty years, from 1836 to 1980, France's Bibliothèque Nationale kept its extensive collection of libertine novels out of the reach of ordinary readers by creating a restricted catalogue known as 'Enfer'.[30] In 1980, several hundred books, previously kept under lock and key, were returned to the library's main collections.

The gradual relaxation of obscenity laws from the 1950s onward meant that maverick editors felt free to try their hand at publishing some of these still proscribed works. But in order to do so, they had to exercise tact and discretion. Maurice Saillet's scholarly edition of *Margot* does not give the name of the house that published it.[31] Rather, it was brought out in the subscription-only 'Cercle du

---

[24] Fougeret de Monbron, *Margot la ravaudeuse, et ses aventures galantes* (Paris: Lenoire, 1784).

[25] Fougeret de Monbron, *Margot la conciacalze e le sue avventure galanti* (n.p.: Biblioteca galante, 1861).

[26] Fougeret de Monbron, *La Brunette ou Avantures d'une Demoiselle* (Amsterdam: n. pub., 1761).

[27] Fougeret de Monbron, *Fanchette, danseuse de l'Opéra, histoire galante* (London/Paris: n. pub., 1796).

[28] See United States Supreme Court, '*Three Censorship Cases*: Memoirs V. Massachusetts 383 U. S. 413, Ginzburg V. United States 383 U. S. 463, Mishkin V. New York 383 U. S. 502' (New York: Chandler Publishing Company, 1966). The outcome of *1966 Memoirs v. Massachusetts 383 U.S. 413* authorized the publication of Cleland's *Fanny Hill*. <https://supreme.justia.com/cases/federal/us/383/413/case.html>

[29] Jean-Louis [*sic*] Fougeret de Monbron, *The Amorous Adventures of Margot* and the *Scarlet Sofa*, translated by Mark Alexander and L. E. LaBan, introduction by Hilary E. Holt (North Hollywood: Brandon House, 1967). <http://scissors-and-paste.net/Brandon_House.html>

[30] Pascal Pia, *Les Livres de l'enfer, bibliographie critique des ouvrages érotiques dans leurs différentes éditions du XVIe siècle à nos jours* (Paris: Courlet et Faure, 2 vols, 1978); re-edited in 1 volume (Paris: Fayard, 1998).

[31] Maurice Saillet (1914–1990): French critic, bibliographer, and man of letters associated in the 1930s and 1940s with Shakespeare and Company and Sylvia Beach.

livre précieux', a semi-clandestine press created in 1958 by Claude Tchou.[32] That same year, the controversial publisher Jean-Jacques Pauvert,[33] known for his 1947 edition of the *Histoire de Juliette* by the marquis de Sade, openly reissued Saillet's *Margot*. That edition was re-printed in 1965. A further edition of *Margot la ravaudeuse* was published in 1972 by the 'Cercle européen du livre', but again without naming an actual publisher, and with the precautionary note on its dust jacket: '*réservé aux adultes*'.

By the early 1980s, the rehabilitation of the libertine novel as an acceptable literary genre was well under way. Between 1984 and 1988 Fayard brought out a seven-volume twenty-nine-novel set, complete with scholarly introductions and illustrations.[34] That was followed in 1993 by Raymond Trousson's 1400-page anthology, which included *Margot la ravaudeuse* and a dozen or so other texts. More recently, in 2000, the prestigious Bibliothèque de la Pléiade published a two-volume set entitled *Romanciers libertins du XVIIIe siècle*, in which they included works by Duclos, Godard d'Aucour, La Morlière, Voisenon, Boyer d'Argens, Chevrier, Dorat, Andréa de Nerciat, Vivant Denon, and, naturally, Fougeret de Monbron.

Viewed alongside major works such as Crébillon's *Les Égarements du cœur et de l'esprit* (1736), or Laclos's *Dangerous Liaisons* (1782), the titles published by Gallimard make up a compendium of bestselling eighteenth-century pornography. One interesting question arises: what does France's literary 'Hell' tell us about the history of thought?

At the very least, the libertine novel allows us to view traditional Enlightenment values such as anticlericalism, rationalism, and individualism from a fresh vantage point. Robert Darnton, among others, has argued that from the 1730s onward, the libertine novel introduced readers to new codes of behaviour, and new ways of thinking.[35] Libertine writers, he claims, portrayed freedom of thought and action by depicting moral depravity and the pursuit of pleasure. Because of its aggressive anticlerical/anti-establishment stance, Darnton credits France's Grub Street with undermining both the Church and the Crown in the years before the French Revolution.[36] Even when reduced to an expression of sexual emancipation

[32] Claude Tchou (1923–2010): French publisher of Belgian-Chinese extraction, Tchou was prosecuted in the 1950s for his edition of Restif de la Bretonne's *Anti-Justine*.

[33] Jean-Jacques Pauvert (1926–2014): French publisher known for publishing the work of the marquis de Sade in the early 1950s and as the first publisher of the *Histoire d'O* (1954).

[34] *L'Enfer de la Bibliothèque Nationale*, 7 vols (Paris: Fayard, 1984–1988).

[35] Robert Darnton, 'Political Sex: Pornography in Old Regime France', in *Enlightenment, Passion, Modernity: Historical Essays in European Thought*, ed. by Mark S. Micale, Robert L. Dietle and Peter Gay (Stanford: Stanford University Press, 2000), pp. 88–112.

[36] See also Marc-André Bernier, *Libertinage et figures du savoir: rhétorique et roman libertin dans la France des Lumières — 1734–1751* (Quebec / Paris: Presses de l'Université Laval / L'Harmattan, 2001), pp. 217–38.

or wanton licentiousness, the libertine novel overtly attacked social and religious prohibitions in the name of personal freedom.[37] For Raymond Trousson, so-called philosophical pornography was an important (and conscious) act of transgression.

On the other side of the English Channel and in America, scholarly interest in libertine literature has steadily grown since the publication of Bradford Mudge's 2000 monograph, *The Whore's Story: Women, Pornography, and the British Novel, 1684–1830*,[38] and his 2004 work *When Flesh Becomes Word: An Anthology of Early Eighteenth-Century Libertine Literature*,[39] as well as Laura Rosenthal's 2008 anthology *The Nightwalkers: Prostitute Narratives from the Eighteenth Century*.[40]

Both Mudge and Rosenthal write that fictional prostitution autobiography has Renaissance and seventeenth-century roots. *Margot* itself references Aretino's *Ragionamenti* (1534–1536), a fictional dialogue between an old prostitute and a novice. The renewed vogue for this sub-genre in the 1740s can be plausibly traced to Antoine Bret's *La Belle Allemande, ou les galanteries de Thérèse* (1745).[41] Bret's novel is an erotic fantasy in which an innocent girl is introduced to prostitution by her own mother. A first-person narrative, part erotica, part social satire, *La Belle Allemande* paints Paris as the undisputed capital of the demi-monde. It is a city where a girl with a pretty face, a neat figure and some native cunning can climb the social ladder to wealth and prosperity.

Following the success of Bret's novel, in 1748 the marquis d'Argens published his sensational *Thérèse philosophe*.[42] Like *La Belle Allemande*, *Thérèse philosophe* is explicitly pornographic, containing scenes of voyeurism, female masturbation, coitus, anal penetration and flagellation, all of which feature prominently in *Margot* as well. Half *femme savante*, half prostitute, Thérèse is a transparent projection of the male erotic imagination. Notwithstanding this, in the second half of the novel female prostitutes stand as a powerful symbol of repressed and abused womanhood. Anticlerical in tone, *Thérèse philosophe* takes aim at forced celibacy and the sexual exploitation of young women by lecherous churchmen.

---

[37] Raymond Trousson, *Les Romans libertins du XVIIIe siècle* (Paris: Éditions Robert Laffont, 2001), p. vii. See 'Libertin/Libertinage': <http://www.bon-a-tirer.com/volume8/rt.html>.

[38] Bradford K. Mudge, *The Whore's Story: Women, Pornography, and the British Novel, 1684–1830* (Oxford: Oxford University Press, 2000). See also Mathilde Cortey, *L'Invention de la courtisane au XVIIIe siècle dans les romans-mémoires des 'filles du monde' de Madame Meheust à Sade: 1732–1797* (Paris: Éditions Arguments, 2001).

[39] Bradford K. Mudge, *When Flesh Becomes Word: An Anthology of Early Eighteenth-Century Libertine Literature* (Oxford: Oxford University Press, 2004).

[40] Laura Rosenthal, *The Nightwalkers: Prostitute Narratives from the Eighteenth Century* (Peterborough: Broadview, 2008).

[41] Antoine Bret, *La Belle Allemande, ou les galanteries de Thérèse* (Amsterdam: Zacharie Chatelin, 1745).

[42] Jean-Baptiste Boyer d'Argens, *Thérèse philosophe, ou Mémoires pour servir à l'histoire du P. Dirrag et de Mlle Éradice, avec l'histoire de Mme Bois-Laurier* (n.p. [La Haye?]: n. pub., 1748).

Along with scenes of intense depravity, the novel also touches on certain philosophical questions such as the moral implications of Cartesian materialism.

Scholars have posited that *Thérèse philosophe* was a composite work, and that the *Story of Manon*, interpolated in the novel's second volume (*Histoire de Madame Bois-Laurier*), was written by our own Monbron.[43] Manon's story clearly adumbrates Margot's tribulations in Mme Florence's bawdy-house at the beginning of *Margot la ravaudeuse*. Following this, several key narrative details can be found in both books. Particularly revealing are the novels' shared *mises-en-scène* where the older woman prepares the younger for her first encounter. But there are other common anecdotes as well, including a disgusting scene in which a punter spews vomit in his prostitute's face. The stories' dovetailing is certainly no coincidence, although the analogies noted do not prove that Monbron had a hand in writing the *Bois-Laurier* segment of *Thérèse philosophe*. For one thing, *Thérèse* and *Margot* are not written in the same style. Monbron's wit is acerbic; all his writings reflect his singular personality. *Thérèse*, on the contrary, is dispassionately written, the novel's restrained style creating its shocking effect. Restraint, we know, was never Monbron's strong suit. In addition to their differing tone, we can find no telling expressions common to the two works that might lead one to suppose that they were written by the same person. The stories convey some similar anecdotes, but their tone and expression are not the same. Finally, *Thérèse philosophe* was in print five years before *Margot*. It seems therefore entirely plausible that Monbron was familiar with the earlier novel, and that he drew on it when writing his own work. As we shall see, *Margot* also incorporates a series of anecdotes and expressions borrowed from Cleland's *Fanny Hill*.

In the wake of *Thérèse philosophe* the confessions-of-a-prostitute genre carried over well into the 1750s. *Les Dégoûts du plaisir* (1752), *Les Égarements de Julie* (1755) and Paul Baret's *Mademoiselle Javotte* (1757) all present variations on the same basic story.[44] The prostitute-heroine-narrator is a pretty girl turned out of doors, sometimes pimped by her own mother (or mother-surrogate). Often, she is seduced by an unscrupulous older man, and not uncommonly by a monk or a priest. Considered alongside *Thérèse philosophe*, these last novels are remarkable in that they present striking similarities to *Margot la ravaudeuse* in theme, tone, and narrative detail. For instance, all include a rogues' gallery of stereotypical characters whose grotesque appearance is the outward sign of their cynicism and moral decay. Bankers, tax collectors, aristocratic rakes and clergymen are the stock characters of these tales. The theme of male homosexuality is also touched

---

[43] Boussuge, pp. 71–164.

[44] *Les Dégoûts du plaisir* (Lampsaque [Paris]: [Duchesne], 1752); Jacques-Antoine-René Perrin, *Les Égarements de Julie* (Paris: Hochereau, 1755); Paul Baret, *Mademoiselle Javotte*, ouvrage moral écrit par elle-même et publié par une de ses amies (La Haye: n.pub., 1757).

upon. *Les Dégoûts du plaisir* presents an explicit scene of sodomy between men. *Margot* hints at male sodomy in the curious scene where she loses her 'other maidenhead' to a ridiculously powdered and scented judge.

Besides the French novels just mentioned (some published after *Margot*), key scenes from *Margot la ravaudeuse* demonstrate the writer's familiarity with English fiction of the period as well, and most notably Cleland's *Fanny Hill* (1748).[45] As previously mentioned, Monbron actually adapted *Fanny Hill* into French and published it in 1751. Unlike French pornography of this period, Cleland's novel is devoid of anticlerical sentiment. The world in which Fanny moves is miles above the sordid reality of street prostitution portrayed in segments of *Margot*. Here and there is a hint of the dangers that might befall the prostitute were she unlucky or unwise. But on the whole, Cleland is unconcerned with exploitation or brutality, and even less with illness, old age, or for that matter pregnancy. The procuress, Mrs Cole, holds that 'pleasure, of one sort or other, [is] the universal port of destination, and every wind that [blows] thither is a good one, provided it [blows] nobody any harm' (p. 236). Like *Thérèse philosophe*, Cleland's novel is a paean to hedonism.

Fanny Hill is indeed remarkable in that the only cautionary note it sounds is aimed at young men in whom dissipation and debauchery undermine even the most robust constitution. Within the context of our novels, the inevitable consequence of a young man's dissolute life is a drained and cadaverous appearance (e.g. Mr Norbert in *Fanny Hill*). The belief that too-frequent emission of semen drains away vital energy was widespread, even in recent times. Generally speaking, the authors of the period issued no such caution for women of pleasure who are portrayed as receptors of the male's vital energy. Margot herself argues that a vigorous sex life, above and beyond the physical demands of her profession, is the key to good health and happiness. Nevertheless, she does fall prey to a mysterious lethargy at the end of the novel not unlike the disorder observed in Cleland's dissipated young men. The cause, we are told: a surfeit of pleasure.

There are strong reasons to believe that when writing *Margot*, Monbron adapted a number of anecdotes from *Fanny Hill*. For example, Cleland's corpulent and middle-aged Mrs Brown has a clear counterpart in *Margot*'s Mme Thomas, whose tremendous breasts and belly hang down to conceal her pudendum, making penetration difficult. The inspiration Monbron found in *Fanny Hill* can also be evidenced by the following passage and the verbal linkage it provides with Monbron's stocking darner Margot.

[45] John Cleland, *Memoirs of a Woman of Pleasure* (Fanny Hill), with an introduction for modern readers by Peter Quennel (New York: Putnam, 1963). All references are to this edition.

> One morning then, that both Mrs Cole and Emily were gone out for the day, and only Louisa and I (not to mention the house-maid) were left in charge of the house, whilst we were loitering away the time in looking through the shop windows, the son of a poor woman, *who earned very hard bread indeed by mending stockings, in a stall in the neighbourhood*, offer'd us some nosegays, ring'd round a small basket; by selling of which the poor boy eked out his mother's maintenance of them both: nor was he fit for any other way of livelihood, since he was not only a perfect changeling, or idiot, but stammer'd so that there was no understanding even those sounds his half dozen, at most, animal ideas prompted him to utter (p. 258) [my italics].

Cleland's description of this unfortunate young man plausibly foreshadows Margot's first love with the stable boy Pierrot. In *Fanny Hill*, Good-natured Dick can be viewed as a prototype of Margot's groom, 'well made, stout, clean-limb'd, tall of his age, as strong as a horse and, withal, pretty featur'd', in spite of being an idiot. Further evidence of *Fanny Hill*'s influence on Monbron is found in the scene where Margot and Pierrot consecrate their love: 'a dingy cabaret furnished only with a broken table and rickety chairs'. Identical furnishings, indeed the same general atmosphere of neglect, characterize the scene recounting Fanny's tryst with a sailor in a docklands tavern, where 'we found no conveniency to our purpose, two or three disabled chairs and a rickety table composing the whole furniture of the room' (p. 231). Lastly, the scene where Fanny observes the two young homosexuals through a peephole in a flimsy partition bears remarkable similarity to the scene in which Margot watches Mme Thomas and Frère Alexis through a peephole that she, like Fanny, actually cuts through the paper partition dividing the room: 'I withdrew to a small closet whose walls were little more than a partition with gaps an inch wide, papered over. Cutting a small hole in the paper, I had a front row seat and could watch their manoeuvres unobserved'. In *Fanny Hill*:

> [t]he partition of our rooms was one of those moveable ones that, when taken down, serv'd occasionally to lay them into one, for the conveniency of a large company; and now, my nicest search could not shew me the shadow of a peep-hole, a circumstance which probably had not escap'd the review of the parties on the other side, whom much it stood upon not to be deceived in it; but at length I observed a paper patch of the same colour as the wainscot, which I took to conceal some flaw: but then it was so high, that I was obliged to stand upon a chair to reach it, which I did as softly as possibly, and, with a point of a bodkin, soon pierc'd it. And now, applying my eye close, I commanded the room perfectly, and could see my two young sparks romping and pulling one another about, entirely, to my imagination, in frolic and innocent play (pp. 254–55).

The concordances we have noted suggest that Monbron's novel echoes in several parts both *Thérèse philosophe* and *Fanny Hill*. And yet in spite of these obvious similarities *Margot la ravaudeuse* presents important and fundamental differences when read alongside the works that influenced it.

In terms of temperament, firstly, Margot, Thérèse and Fanny illustrate opposing philosophical inclinations. Margot is a born cynic. The convent-bred Thérèse, on the other hand, is an epicurean who actually becomes ill when deprived of carnal pleasure. And whereas Thérèse is of solid bourgeois stock, and Fanny a simple country girl, Margot is emphatically a back-street child of the city. Born and bred in the east end of Paris, Margot's world is that of the raucous *petit peuple*: soldiers, porters, hawkers, tinkers, chair menders. Her journey from east to west is a symbolic odyssey taking her from poverty and obscurity to wealth and fame. In the 1760s readers would have immediately grasped how Margot's journey prophesied the career of the great royal mistress Madame Du Barry (1743–1793). Thus the narrator may claim that he wishes to 'portray [the harlot] in the worst possible light, and to have her slowly pass through the most abominable trials'; however, the reader might be forgiven for not apprehending that aim. To be sure, Monbron gives Margot's tribulations ample treatment. Her spectacular rise passes through three distinctive steps, each punctuated by disastrous setbacks, including prison and venereal infection. Her career is nevertheless a great success. Throughout, the novel's mainspring is its heroine's instinct for survival, untroubled by conscience or constraint. For a poor girl without adequate family connections, prostitution is the key, and the only key, to the moneyed world of judges, merchants, high churchmen, noblemen, financiers, and, ultimately, freedom. In her dealings with men, the young prostitute displays a disconcerting ruthlessness all her own. The girl wishing to live off her charms is given the following cold-hearted advice: she must 'set her sights on her own interest and profits'.

Leaving aside the novel's obscenity, *Margot la ravaudeuse* must also be singled out for the way in which it bridges English and French literature at an interesting crossroads in their parallel histories. During the decade before *Margot*'s publication and long after, French critics frequently censured the English 'domestic' novel for its trivial tone and vulgarity. Partisans of a refined and elevated literary decorum, French writers held the view that the novel should respect the prescriptions of polite society. Fielding's novels, in particular *Joseph Andrews* (1742) and *Tom Jones* (1749), were criticized for their low humour. 'Cat fights', slapstick scenes of mistaken identity, drunkenness, lewd behaviour, and fisticuffs ruffled élite French sensibilities. *Margot la ravaudeuse* was never going to be taken up by polite society. It is nevertheless interesting to note how the novel, for all its technical flaws, reinterprets the stock scenes of English comic fiction made famous by Fielding, and introduced to French readers by the translators abbé Desfontaines and Pierre-Antoine de La Place. Monbron's fascination with English manners can be evidenced by *Margot*'s female brawl, its description of bouts of boxing, and the disapproving account it gives of English domestic life: swearing, belching, unappetising meals (roasted meats and butter-soaked cabbage served with apple marmalade), not to forget the ubiquitous punch bowl, tobacco and pipes.

At the time *Margot* was published, the vogue for sentimental romance, largely inspired by Richardson's *Pamela*, was in the ascendant. A century later, virtually all fiction was coloured with the sentimental, *larmoyant* sensibility. A nineteenth-century novelist would have had Margot end her career as a tragic figure, ill, destitute and full of remorse, like Marguerite a century later in the last pages of Dumas's *La Dame aux camélias* (1848). Instead of which Monbron ultimately portrays Margot as the epitome of respectability: serene, happy, and rich. It is not often pointed out, but unlike seventeenth- and nineteenth-century French literature, eighteenth-century literature is not memorable for its female characters. Margot's rival in the mid-eighteenth century is also her most obvious foil. Prévost's Manon Lescaut, for all her frivolity, is the symbol of love — true, heartfelt, but ill-fated. Her pathetic story was replayed countless times in art and literature. By contrast, Margot's defiance of love and Fate, and her instinct for self-preservation, place her outside the literary canon. Still, it is not for nothing that prostitutes and bankers have been recently considered as living 'metaphors of modernity'.[46] In this sense Margot must be seen as a forerunner of Balzac's courtesans and, early in the twentieth century, of Proust's Odette de Crécy. Unconstrained by moralising, Margot speaks the language of commerce, not love.

In English literature, Margot has an even closer descendant in Catherine Gore's *The Tale of a Tub* (1837) in which the stocking mender Jeannette becomes the rival of the royal mistress, Madame Du Barry.[47] The play eschews obscenity, but its main elements bear an uncanny resemblance to Monbron's novel, including the following paraphrase: 'I'm told you're the best taker up of a stitch in Paris' (p. 303). How did the staunchly middle-class Catherine Gore learn of *Margot la ravaudeuse*?

Yet another of Margot's English offspring may well be Thackeray's Becky Sharp. Let us recall that that compelling young woman was the daughter of a poor artist and a glamorous 'French opera girl' (a prostitute). Selfish and aggressive, Becky Sharp is called upon to act the part of modesty, simplicity, gentleness and untiring good humour with the consummate skill of an actress. She is not exactly a prostitute, but her objective, like Margot's, is simple: to carve out a place in Vanity Fair, whatever the cost; and like Margot, she succeeds.

Édouard Langille

---

[46] Maurice Samuels, 'Metaphors of Modernity: Prostitutes, Bankers, and Other Jews in Balzac's *Splendeurs et Misères Des Courtisanes*', *The Romanic Review*, 97, 2 (March 2006), pp. 169–84.

[47] C. Gore, *The Tale of a Tub*, in *Gore on Stage: The Plays of Catherine Gore*, ed. by John Franceschina (New York/London: Garland Publishing, 2005), pp. 298–317.

NOTES ON THE PRESENT TRANSLATION

My translation is based on Maurice Saillet's authoritative 1958 edition of *Margot la ravaudeuse*, published by Claude Tchou and Jean-Jacques Pauvert. Saillet's text does not present significant variants with more recent editions (Trousson 1993, Delon 1993, Wald Lasowski 2000, Seth 2010). All reproduce the 1753 Hamburg edition (dated 1800) which is the only edition of *Margot* published during the author's lifetime: MARGOT LA RAVAUDEUSE / Par Mr. de M**. / A HAMBOURG. / M. D. C. C. C.

Monbron annotated his original text. I have reproduced his twenty-six notes, marked §. My own notes are indicated by Arabic numerals and are placed at the end of the text.

Since *Margot* is set in France, French honorifics and names have been left untouched. Aristocratic titles and toponyms respect French orthography, hyphenation and punctuation: duc rather than Duc, rue Sainte-Anne and not St Anne Street. Likewise, all personal titles are written in unabbreviated French: Monsieur, not M., Madame not Mme, and so forth. The word *abbé* literally means 'abbot', but in eighteenth-century France the term frequently referred to clerics who had been tonsured and wore dark robes and clerical collars but had not necessarily received consecration.

Margot is a prostitute. Monbron uses a number of terms to signify the women who exercise that profession: *catin*, *fille*, *fille entretenue*, *fille du monde*, *demoiselle du monde*, *actrice*. Likewise, prostitution is referred to as *la profession de fille du monde*, and the world of prostitution is *le petit monde* or *le monde galant*. For these expressions and others I have tried to use English equivalents with a period ring: whore, naturally, but also bawd, harlot, strumpet, kept woman, courtesan, fancy lady or even streetwalker, depending on the context.

The geography of Paris plays an important role in the novel. Margot's journey takes her from the working-class east of the city westward to the seats of wealth and power. Having amassed enough money to keep a proper house, Margot repairs to an unnamed suburb where she retires in peace and quiet. I have accordingly tried to identify neighbourhoods, suburbs and relevant street names.

Currency always poses translation difficulties, especially in period texts. For paltry sums I do not hesitate to use rough English equivalents: *sol/sou* = a penny, twopence, threepence, sixpence (*huit sous*) and farthing (*obole*). For larger sums I maintain the French values where *livre* is marked *l.* For conversion's sake, the *louis d'or* can be considered the equivalent of a guinea. English characters spend English currency.

- *louis d'or* (gold coin) = 24 *livres*, along with a half-louis coin (the *demi-louis d'or*) and a two-louis coin (the *double louis d'or*) (12 and 48 *livres*). The *livre tournois*, or *franc*, was, in common with the original *livre* of Charlemagne, divided into 20 *sols* (*sous* after 1715), each of which was divided into 12 *deniers*.
- *écu* (silver coin) = 6 *livres* = 120 *sols*, along with ½, ¼ and ⅛ *écu* denominations (60, 30 and 15 *sols*)
- copper coins of 1 and 2 *sols*: 1 *sol* = 12 *deniers*
- 6 and 3 *deniers* (the latter also called a *liard*) were also issued.

Lastly, I would like to thank David Blewett, Earla Wilputte, Suzanne Stewart, Alison Finch and Peter Urbach for their helpful comments and encouragement.

É. L.

Fougeret de Monbron
(1706–1760)

Margot la ravaudeuse

Translated with an introduction and notes
by Édouard M. Langille

Here at last is *Margot la ravaudeuse*, a novel which General de la Pousse,§[1] encouraged by the corporation of harlots and their infamous henchmen, would have us believe constitutes a crime against the State. The author, accused of nothing less than having attempted to undermine the authority of religion, the government and the Sovereign, and fearing that his silence was in itself an admission of guilt, he had no choice but to publish the work, leaving the question of guilt or innocence entirely in the hands of the public.

§ Police Inspector.

Margot la ravaudeuse

It is not because of vanity, and even less for reasons of modesty, that I reveal the many parts I played in my youth. Rather, my goal is, if at all possible, to check the vanity of those women who made their fortune the same way I did. I also wish to offer the public a word of thanks, as, indeed, I am wholly indebted to public generosity for all the luxuries I now enjoy.

I was born in the rue Saint-Paul[2] of the illicit union of an honest soldier and a stocking darner. My mother, who was naturally lazy, taught me as a child how to darn socks and mend old clothes. Her goal was to send me out to work as soon as possible in order to live off my earnings. When I reached the age of thirteen, she turned her barrel[§] over to me on condition that at the end of each day, I turn my earnings over to her. She then passed over her list of clients. I soon fulfilled her expectations. Before long I was the best stocking darner in the neighbourhood. Nor did I confine my talents to taking in stockings and trousers. I soon learned how to mend old drawers and, especially, how to patch the seat. What complemented my success in the mending trade was the pretty face that nature had bestowed upon me. Before long, everyone for miles around wanted to be patched up by me. Thus my little tub became the *rendezvous* of all the neighbouring footmen. It was in this brilliant company that I made my first *entrée* into society; for, if the truth be told, it was in the rue Saint-Antoine[3] that I first acquired the social graces that I perfected only once I made my way in the wider world.

I inherited a natural disposition for carnal pleasure and was eager to experience the joys of love for myself. My father, my mother and I lived in a single fourth-floor room, sparsely furnished with two cane-bottomed chairs, some broken crockery, an old wardrobe and an ugly old bed without curtains, let alone a tester.[4] It was in this bed that we three slept.

Once I reached puberty, I began to sleep less soundly. I noticed from time to time that my bed-fellows toyed with each other in the most curious fashion. Nay, they sometimes took to bouncing about with such vigour that the bed rocked furiously. I bounced along. Soon they were panting and whispering words of endearment. Awakened by their lovemaking, my soul was on fire. I was in a cold sweat. I could not draw a breath. Overcome by the idea of love, I was truly beside

---

[§] Most Parisian stocking darners work in a barrel or a tub.

myself. I became so jealous of my mother's fits of pleasure that I wanted to strike her. Under the circumstances what could I do? Pleasuring myself offered the only outlet for the feelings aroused in me. Fortunately enough, I was not inclined to finger cramps. I instinctively knew that such solitary recreation was mere child's play compared to the real thing. I nonetheless spent hours at it without the slightest satisfaction. I managed only to whip my soul into an even greater frenzy of desire. In short, I had the very devil in my skin. A fine kettle of fish, you might say, for a fourteen-year-old girl. But I ask, was it entirely my fault? The apple does not fall far from the tree, as the expression goes. My flesh was tortured by frustrated desire; little surprise, then, that I should try to find a lover capable of satisfying my yearnings.

Among the numerous flunkies whose homage I was accustomed to receiving, there was one young well-made stable boy who seemed worthy of consideration. He paid me a charming compliment after the manner of a stable boy, by claiming that he never rubbed down a horse without thinking of me. To which I responded that I never mended a pair of drawers without daydreaming of my Pierrot (for such was his name). We paid each other many compliments, none of which I can recall. The important thing was that in a short while Pierrot and I agreed to consecrate our love with the seal of Cythera[5] in a dingy little cabaret near la Rapée.[6] The room was furnished with a rickety table and a few broken chairs; the walls were covered from ceiling to floor with scandalous graffiti drawn in charcoal by the drunks and ruffians who hung about the place. Our meal was accordingly very simple: a sixpenny bottle of wine, and twopence worth of cheese and bread. We nevertheless supped with as much ceremony as we would have done *chez Duparc*[§] for a *louis d'or*. The simplest food is scrumptious when seasoned with love.

At last, we came to the matter at hand. The problem was where to get settled. It would have been ill-advised to lie on the table or to lean against the chairs. We decided to try standing up. Pierrot pushed me against the wall. Almighty Priapus![7] What a fright I had when he undid his flies and I first perceived the raging monster betwixt his legs! And what of the thumping and banging once he tried to take me? The walls shook with the strain. I too was shaking with anticipation. I even tried my best to give the lad a hand, not wanting him to have to do all the work. In spite of our best efforts, Pierrot was still not out of, or rather, in the gate.

I was beginning to despair that we would not meet with the success I had dreamt of when it occurred to Pierrot to wet his throbbing engine with some spittle. Oh nature! How admirable are your secrets. No sooner had he wet his prick than the little path to joy opened. He shot in, and I was well and truly deflowered. I can say no more about it save that from that point onward I had no

---

[§] Head chef at the *Hôtel de Ville*.

trouble falling asleep. A thousand pleasant dreams accompanied my slumber. Monsieur and Madame Tranche-montagne (my parents) were free to rock the bed to their heart's delight. I no longer heard their frolics.

Our innocent turtle billing and cooing lasted for about a year. I loved Pierrot and he loved me. He was perfection incarnate. I could find no fault in him, save that he was poor, a gambler, and a drunkard. They say that friends must share and share alike, so I covered his debts. A stable boy would rather eat his own currycomb than rely on anyone else. Pierrot, on the contrary, was so miserly with his own money that he soon spent all mine. Before long, I lost my barrel and with it, my place in the darning trade. My mother had for some time been aware that my work was not bringing in as much money as had formerly been the case, and she gave me a proper scolding. The cat was not long out of the bag. Before long she discovered where all my money was going. For a time she kept it to herself. Then one morning, when I was still fast asleep, my good mother armed herself with a new broom and quietly removed my shift. She proceeded to give me a terrible thrashing. Before I knew what was going on, my buttocks were covered with blood. I tried to get away, but I could not escape the swinging broom. What a humiliation for an honest working girl like me, whipped like a little child! I was so incensed that I decided then and there to break out on my own. I made up my mind and, taking advantage of my mother's turned back, I dressed in my Sunday best and quietly bade farewell to Madame Tranche-montagne and her humble abode forever.

I walked down to the *Grève*[8] and then followed the river as far as the *Pont Royal*[9] where I entered into the Tuileries.[10] I ambled round the garden without really knowing what I was doing. I had calmed down by that point and decided to sit awhile near the *Terrace des Capucins.*[11] I sat there for a few minutes daydreaming when a small well-dressed lady,[12] very proper in every way, sat down beside me. We greeted one another and began talking of nothing, really.

— My goodness, Mademoiselle, do you not mind the heat?
— Very warm, Madame, very warm. Happily there is a light breeze.
— Very happily indeed, my dear. What crowds there will be at Saint-Cloud[13] if this heat persists.
— Indeed, Madame, the crowds will be prodigious.
— But, Mademoiselle, have we not met before? Did I not have the pleasure of making your acquaintance in Brittany?
— No Madame, I have never been out of Paris.
— 'pon my word, yes, I declare. You look just like a young girl I met in Nantes. One would swear… Indeed, a very pretty girl she was too… such a lovely girl.
— You are very kind, Madame, I don't think I'm that pretty. You are kind to say so just the same. After all, what good is a pretty face?

Uttering this last phrase I sighed and could not help shedding a few tears.

— My dear child, said she, taking me by the hand, you're crying. Prithee, tell me what's the matter? What has happened that makes you so unhappy? Speak, my pretty one. Don't be afraid. Open your heart to me. You can count on my compassion. Rest assured that I will do anything I can to help. There, there, my sweet, there, let's go for a little walk. Shall we? Let's get a bite to eat at Madame Lacroix's?[§14] What do you say? There, you can tell me all about it. I can perhaps be more help than you think.

I was easily persuaded, especially as I hadn't had anything to eat all day. I followed her, convinced that my lucky star had sent a guardian angel whose wise counsel would save me from the dangers of living out-of-doors. After two cups of steaming white coffee and a couple of rolls, I told her where I was from and explained my profession. In this I was entirely truthful, but I thought it prudent to blame my mother for my present predicament. In order to justify my having run away, I made my mother out to be a true harridan.

— Good Heavens! cried my charitable and yet still nameless protectoress. What a sin to force a pretty girl like to you to work in such deplorable conditions, to be exposed year in and year out to all types of weather, to suffer heat and cold bent over in a barrel, and to have to mend wretched old worn-out clothes. No, my princess, you're not cut out for that kind of drudgery. When one is as pretty as you are, one can reasonably aim for something better. In no time I could make something out of you… if…
— My good lady, what can I do? Tell me! Help me! I put myself completely in your hands.
— Well, to start with, you can move in with me. I already have four girls who pay their way. You'll be the fifth.
— But, my good lady, have you forgotten that I haven't a farthing to my name? How can I pay for room and board?
— Don't let's worry about that. For the time being, all that is required is that you do exactly as I ask. Just leave everything to me. I'll let you in on a little business interest of mine. God willing, before the end of the month, you will be in a position to cover the cost of living under my roof, and you'll have plenty of spending money besides.

I was so overcome with gratitude that I almost fell to my knees with tears of joy. I couldn't wait to find out what this was all about. Thanks to my lucky star, I did

---

[§] Formerly ran the café in the Tuileries.

not have long to wait. The clock chimed midday. We left the Tuileries through the *Porte des Feuillants*[15] where an elegant carriage was waiting to whisk us off toward the boulevards and thence, to a remote house situated off the rue Montmartre.[16]

The house itself resembled a sort of hermitage wedged between courtyard and garden. A pretty house, I recall, and one which gave such a favourable impression of its inhabitants that I found myself feeling grateful for my mother's barbaric treatment earlier that same morning. It was true, I told myself, that running away had led to my fortunate encounter with my kind new friend.

We entered a pleasantly furnished ground-floor room. The other residents soon appeared. Their stylish almost coquettish appearance and forward manners made me so uncomfortable that I was unable to speak or even to look them in the eye, managing only a few words to acknowledge their civilities. My benefactress instantly guessed that my shabby clothes were the cause of my embarrassment; she promised that I would soon be turned out just as elegantly as the other girls. It is true that I was profoundly mortified to have nothing better to wear than a tawdry grey dress, especially in the company of young women whose petticoats were cut out of the finest Indian and French cloth.

I began to wonder, not without some trepidation, what kind of business I was on the point of taking up. While I was still trying to solve the puzzle, we were called to the table and supper was served. The food, which was not at all bad, was seasoned by the high spirits of those in attendance. We tucked in with such voracious appetites that below stairs the servants lost hope of licking our plates. Need I add that in order to avoid choking, we drank copious amounts of wine? Everything was going wonderfully well when all of a sudden two of the girls, the worse for drink, got into a scuffle, one punching the other in the chops, the second firing a plate at the first. In a flash, the table, the crockery, the food, everything was flying through the air. War had been declared. Our two heroines were at each other's throats with equal fury. Escoffions,[17] neckerchiefs, lace cuffs, everything was ripped to shreds.[18]

The mistress of the house tried to get a handle on the situation and, in the process, received, quite by accident, a poke in the eye. She was mightily taken aback to have been thus caressed. Losing all self-control, she revealed herself a champion in the heroic arts. There was no longer any question of declaring a truce. The two other girls, who until that moment had remained strictly neutral, decided that the time had come to choose sides, and threw themselves into the melee. From the onset of hostilities I crept into a corner, whence I did not stir. I moved not a muscle until the battle raged no more. And what a battle, at once frightening and comical! To watch five harpies rolling on the floor, hair in their faces, biting, scratching, kicking, punching, caterwauling at the tops of their lungs, screaming the vilest insults, all the while exposing, half naked, their large and their small wares in the most scandalous fashion imaginable! I swear, hostilities would still be on-going today had an old man, who looked as if he had been on the job for donkey's years, not interrupted the afore-described proceedings by announcing the arrival of a German baron. Nothing commands respect like a title. Once the antagonists heard the word 'baron' all hostilities immediately ceased. They straightened up and tried to recover their composure. They wiped their faces and fixed their clothes. Those same faces that were so hideously contorted a few moments earlier, regained their erstwhile expression of sweetness and serenity. The mistress of the house instantly went out to greet the baron; the girls flew to their chambers to change in order to receive their guest decently.

The reader, more astute than I, has already guessed that I was in one of the most respectable houses in the capital. Without my having to repeat the fact, he will know that our hostess, who was in great demand in this particular trade, was called Madame Florence.[19] Once she learned that the baron had only announced himself in order to put a stop to the violent scene just described, she came back to find me, extremely pleased with herself.

— There, there, my pretty, she said, giving me a peck on the forehead, don't let our high spirits give you the wrong impression. It's nothing really, a storm in a teacup, easily settled. We can't always control our feelings. People are touchy, what can one do? If you step on a worm it reacts. Once you get to know the other girls you'll find their sweetness charming. They all have hearts of gold. Their occasional anger quickly passes, and then all is forgotten. Heaven knows, I have no more bitterness than a dove, but God help anyone who crosses me. But let's change the subject. Now, what about you? Everybody agrees, my pretty, that without money we are nothing. As they say: no money, no prayers. One might add, no money, none of life's pleasures: no comfort. Now, since we all like comfort, which you must agree requires money, it would be foolish to refuse to make money however one can, especially when the means are of no harm to anyone. In which case, earning money would be evil, God preserve us. Yes, by all means, God preserve us. On that count, my conscience is clear. I defy anyone to show how I have caused a penny's worth of harm to anyone. Anyhow, we're not living here amongst a band of Arabs; we have to look after our souls. The main point is to be straightforward. It is not against the law to earn one's keep. The choice of career is of no importance so long as it is honest. I think one would be mad not to try and get ahead when one has the chance, and who could be better placed than you, with all the resources nature has bestowed on you? Are you so pretty for nothing? I know so many girls in the trade[§] who, though not as pretty as you, have managed to amass a

[§] 'Demoiselle du monde': euphemism for whore.

considerable private income. I helped them along the way, mind you, not that they remember the fact. May God convert the ingrates! But let's not allow that to spoil our fun.

— My dear lady, I said breathlessly, I hope never to give you cause to complain about my ingratitude.

— Ouf, they all say the same thing, and then they do as they please once they're established. If you only knew how many high-class ladies of pleasure got their start with me, and who now don't even bother to speak, you would concede that gratitude is no longer in fashion. Never mind, it's always nice to be accommodating. Speaking of which, have you ever, how can I put it, have you ever accommodated anyone, my puss?[§]

— Who me, Madame? I answered hypocritically. Who might I have accommodated in my little corner?

— You don't understand. I suppose I have to speak more clearly. Are you still a maid?[20]

The question was so unexpected that my cheeks flushed and I was unable to answer.

— I see, said she, that you are no longer. Have no fear, I have some miraculous ointments.[21] We'll sort it out. Still, I must examine you myself. It's a painless procedure. All girls destined for this trade must undergo an examination. After all, I say, the shopkeeper has to know what's in the shop.

By the time Madame Florence finished this phrase she had already pulled my petticoat up over my thighs. She proceeded to raise my plump buttocks and, turning me over on her knee, nothing escaped her sharp eye.

— Well that's good. Now I am pleased. The damage is slight and can easily be repaired. You have, you can thank your lucky star, one of the loveliest bodies I have ever seen. The day will come, mark my words, when that body will provide for you. It is not, however, enough to be pretty. One must also look after oneself. For instance, it is indispensable not to spare the sponge. Upon inspection, I am not so sure you're familiar with how to use that particular object. Come. Let me show you now that we have a minute.

She led me into a small closet and, sitting me down legs astride, she gave me my first lesson in personal hygiene.

[§] 'Chat': term of endearment in the demi-monde.

We spent the rest of the day preoccupied with trifles of little importance. As promised, the next day I was transformed from head to toe. I was given a pink taffeta dress trimmed with furbelows[22] over a muslin skirt. I had a mock gold watch tied round my waist. I thought I looked stunning in my new dress. Spying myself in the glass, I became aware for the first time of the power of vanity. I contemplated my reflection with respect and admiration.

To be fair, Madame Florence must be revered as a most accomplished high priestess in the Order of Venus. She was on top of everything. Apart from the girls living under her roof who were always on call to service passing trade, she could also call upon reinforcements in the town who were summoned for special occasions. And that is not all. She had a complete wardrobe of dresses in a great many styles and colours, and these she hired for a pretty penny to new recruits like me, that is, over and above her handling fee.

Alert to the exceptional value of novelty in the trade, Madame Florence wasted no time informing her most trusted clients of her find. Her strategy soon paid off. I did not have long to wait before I was introduced to my first trick. His honour Judge —, in truth, more assiduous in pursuing his amorous assignations than he was in making his daily appearance in court, arrived just as I finished dressing. He was a small man, entirely dressed in black, perched on two bird-legs. He stood upright and looked stiff and uncomfortable in his clothes. On his head, which appeared soldered to his shoulders, he wore an expertly curled wig, so caked with powder that his clothes looked like those of the jolly miller. On top of which, he positively reeked of scent. It was all I could do to keep from swooning. Even a perfumer would have fainted.

— Ah, this time you've outdone yourself, Florence, he cried, casting a furtive glance in my direction. This one's what I call beautiful, gorgeous, divine! Yes, by Jove, you've outdone yourself today. Mademoiselle is quite simply adorable. What! What! … a hundred times better looking than what you'd led me to think. She is an angel. I speak the truth, judge's honour. I can't get over it. Such fine eyes. I simply have to kiss them. I cannot contain myself.

Madame Florence could see how things were going; she saw that a third party would be in the way and thought it best to withdraw. As soon as we were alone, the judge, without compromising the dignity of his profession, had me lie on a sofa. For a few moments he relished my beauty. He then touched my nether parts and asked me to turn over. He had me hold a position very different from the one I was used to adopting with Pierrot. He bade me relax. What a dreadful brute! He proceeded to do to me what certain types of gentlemen do to each other. He ravished my other maidenhead![23] Oh, the dreadful contortions I had to endure in this most unnatural position. My agonizing cries soon convinced him that I had taken no pleasure in our little tryst. To reward me for my pains he slipped two *louis d'or* in my hand.

— This, he said, is a little treat for you, a supererogation[24] if you like. Don't mention it to Madame Florence. I'll settle my account with her and throw in a little extra for you. I'll pay her share and yours. Farewell, my little queen. Kiss me before I go. Now, let me kiss your little dimple. There, there, I hope we meet again one day. Yes, I think we will, as I am so pleased with you and with your beautiful manners.

He left quickly with short stiff steps that made the floor squeak.

What had just taken place was so shocking that I knew not what to think. Perhaps the judge simply mistook his aim. On the other hand, perhaps what he did is common among people of rank. If that's the fashion, said I to myself, I suppose I will have to go along with it. I'm no more delicate than the next girl. The first time is always a bit rough, but with practice, one can get used to anything. Lord knows, I got used to Pierrot and his groping, and it wasn't easy in the beginning.

I was rehearsing this little monologue in my head when Madame Florence returned.

— Well, my pretty, she said, rubbing her hands. Is it not true that the judge is an agreeable man? Prithee, did he leave anything for you?
— No, Madame.
— Here's a *louis d'or* that he asked me to give you. Let's hope it won't be the last. He seemed very pleased with you. But be that as it may, my sweet, you must not surmise that all our transactions will be as lucrative as this one. Not all our clients are as generous. You have to take the good with the bad. In business there are good days and bad and, what's more, the good makes up for the bad. There's no trader but meets with losses. La, la, the trade would be a gold mine were it not for the odd punter who doesn't cough up. But patience, my dear, patience. A synod[25] of high-ranking clergy is due to convene. We'll be up to our necks in gold! Joking aside, my house does not have a bad reputation. If I had an income of a thousand a year for every high ranking churchman I have entertained, I could live like a queen. But after all, I can't complain. I have, I thank God, enough to live on. I could stop working altogether. But to be good only for oneself is to be good for nothing. You have to do something. Idleness is the mother of all vice. If everyone had something to do, no one would get into mischief …

During this tedious sermon I could not help yawning. Observing this, Madame Florence sent me to my room recommending that I make use of the bidet.[26]

Let me point out as an aside that respectable women are greatly in the working girl's debt. They owe us, not only the invention of this commodious little receptacle, but also a prodigious number of charming devices whose sole purpose is to enhance nature or to improve upon its imperfections. The harlot teaches the *bourgeoise* how to make the most of her natural graces and how to combine them variously so as to always be seen to best advantage. The lady of pleasure teaches the *bourgeoise* how to walk with grace and ease and to deport herself with elegance. To be sure, respectable women make a proper study of the way we act, of all the little nothings that make us seductive. In a word, though they rail against us, respectable women know that they are desirable only insofar as they have learned to ape our behaviour. Their virtue is inseparable from our sin. Deep down inside, they all have something of the whore. May this little digression serve to raise the dignity of the profession and remind those who run us into the ground to give us our due!

Now, back to my story.

Madame Florence, who had just finished her sermon against idleness, did not leave much time for me to get into trouble. For there she was once again at my door.

— My little sweet, I did not want to bother you so soon, but the other girls are busy with a gang of young sparks I would not feel easy introducing to you. I mean, everything else being equal, they don't always have ready money and, God knows, it's not my intention that you should work for nothing. To make a long story short, I have downstairs a tax collector who's a friend of mine. He's been coming round for years and he pays two *louis d'or* up front. I don't want to let him down. What do you say, my darling? Two gold coins are nothing to sneer at, especially when there's practically no effort to earn them.
— Not as little as you might think, Madame. I was in excruciating pain, just now. I still am. If you had to put up with the ordeal I've just been through! My backside is killing me.
— Oh, everybody's not as rough as our friend the judge. The one I'm proposing just wants a quick squeeze, nothing more. I guarantee that he'll feel you up and that's it. In two shakes of a lamb's tail he'll be off.

Madame Florence finally got my consent. The man she introduced to me was the most hideous-looking tax collector imaginable. Picture this: a square head glued to a porter's shoulders, tired, fearsome eyes under bushy eyebrows, a low wrinkled forehead, a wide triple chin, a pear-shaped belly held up by two heavy bowed legs, and, finally, feet as flat as a duck's. Each part individually, and all parts together, made up this *fiscal* beau. I was so shocked by his appearance, which resembled that of an automaton, that I did not notice the disappearance of our mother superior.

— So what are we supposed to do, stand here with our hands in our pockets? Hem, hem! And you, what are you doing standing there like a booby? Come! Come! Over here! I say, I don't have time to stand here day-dreaming. I'm expected at a meeting. Hem, hem! Let's get a move on. Where is your hand? Now take hold of this here. Squeeze your fingers. Like that. Move your wrists, like that. Just like that. That's it, a little harder, a little… Now stop! Faster! Easy! Easy! Ah! Ah! Good, that's good. Just like that. Ah! Ah!

Once this charming exercise was over, he tossed me a couple of *louis d'or* and then made off as if he were being pursued by creditors.

When I take the time to reflect on the cruel and bizarre treatment a prostitute has to put up with I can scare imagine a viler condition, including that of galley-slave or courtier. Is there anything more disgusting than having to satisfy the fantasies of any Tom, Dick or Harry? To smile at a detestable old fart, to caress someone everyone finds repulsive, to lend our bodies to every imaginable vice, in a word, to hide one's true feelings behind an impenetrable mask in order to laugh, to sing and to drink; to hand oneself over to the wildest excesses, nay, to the most degrading and humiliating acts of wickedness, most often against our will and with extreme reluctance? Those who imagine that the life of a prostitute is a bed of roses don't know the half of it.[27] The courtier, that snivelling despicable slave, who creeps on his belly in the shadow of the great and the good, who manages to hang on at the cost of a thousand humiliations, whose true feelings are forever hidden, the courtier, I say, does not suffer half the trials and tribulations of a whore. I have no difficulty affirming that the whore works for the good of her soul. If our sufferings in this world counted as penance, every whore would have a special place in the bosom of Mother Church. Nay, we would be worthy candidates for canonization. Depraved self-interest greases the wheels of the trade. The whore can expect as her just reward public scorn and brutality. Only a whore knows the true horror of it. I cannot recall my novitiate without trembling. And yet, how many others have had it rougher than I. The triumphant beauty queen who glides through the town in a gilded carriage decorated with the most exquisite paintings, all varnished by Martin,[28] is a living advertisement of her benefactor's perverted taste. Who would believe that this great beauty was once a footman's cast-off, and that she had to put up with the rabble's most brutal treatment? For aught I know she has the scars to prove it. Let me say it again. Our life might seem alluring: nothing could be more humiliating.

Unless you've actually experienced it, you can't imagine how perverted men can be in their pursuit of pleasure. I have known a fair number whose special delight it was to be whipped and then to whip me. Having slapped, spanked and caned some old codger, it was my turn to turn over and suffer the same treatment from him! It must seem odd that there are girls patient enough to put up with this kind of life. Take it from me, lechery, avarice, sloth, and the hope of a better life will lead one to commit the vilest outrages.

For four months, I lived under the care of Madame Florence. I therefore can lay some claim to having successfully completed an advanced course in the world's oldest profession. When I left the school, I could rival the wicked, both Ancient and Modern, in the art of gratifying every desire. In short, I held a master's degree in physical depravity.

However, one instance in particular pushed me over the brink and resolved me to strike out on my own. This is what happened. One day we received the visit of a company of musketeers, as rowdy as they were hard up. Weary that evening of worshipping at the altar of Silenus,[29] in other words, drunk as so many lords, they got it into their heads to honour Venus instead. There were only two of us at home. My colleague had just been prescribed a refrigerative[30] and was out of commission, as it were. I therefore found myself having to service the whole lot on my own. Respectfully, I explained, but in vain, how it was simply impossible to satisfy everyone. Like it or not, I had to do as they commanded. Mercy me, in the space of two hours, I was mounted thirty times. How many pious godly women would like to have traded places with me to earn their eternal reward? As for me, poor sinner that I am, I own that, far from taking things lying down and conferring a silent blessing on my assailants, I flew into a blooming rage, cursing them to their faces until, finally, they left me in peace. It was too much to bear. I was so gorged with pleasure that I was doubled over with stomach cramps.

After this brutal experience, Madame Florence knew that she could not convince me to stay on under her roof. She agreed that we should part, on condition that I might make myself available for special occasions. We parted full of feelings of good will and mutual respect. I bought some clothes and a few sticks of furniture, and set up house in a set of rooms in the rue d'Argentueil,[31] hoping that I might avoid the watchful eye of the authorities. What good is prudence when you're down on your luck? Malicious slander was my downfall. It struck when I expected it least.

Among the sundry rakes who discreetly frequented my boudoir, there was one old growler who blamed me for a certain indisposition which, or so he later claimed, came on all of a sudden some time after we first became acquainted. I denied the accusation with *hauteur*. He was more indignant than ever and ended up creating such a fuss that two local jades, jealous of my success, denounced me to the police. They did their work well. One lovely evening I was rounded up and packed off to *Bicêtre*.[32] The first ceremony was to submit to a physical examination and allow myself to be fingered by a couple of young surgeons who declared me infected with the pox and condemned me, without appeal, to be placed under quarantine *hic et nunc*.[33] Once I was duly bled, purged, and washed, I was rubbed down with efficacious grease.[34] The weight of a thousand tiny particles of mercury dilates the lymph nodes and restores their natural fluidity.

One ought not to be surprised that I am familiar with the terms of the doctor's art. During my stay of more than a month, I had ample opportunity to learn his craft. Then again, a lady of pleasure meets all ranks of men, and learns to talk with authority on any number of subjects. Is there any profession whose jargon we do not learn? The soldier, the lawyer, the financier, the philosopher, the clergyman — men from all walks of life seek our company. Each speaks the jargon of his own profession. How, I ask, with so many ways to become learned, could we manage not to do so?

During my incarceration at *Bicêtre*, I was pleased to make the acquaintance of several girls whose names I won't repeat, out of respect for their protectors, amongst whom we would recognize several of the kingdom's grandest noblemen, all in the thrall of common harlots. There are people whose rank we must perforce respect, in spite of their manifold wickedness. It is surely not for us to censure the good and the great. If a man of rank prefers the companionship of a vile strumpet to more refined company, that's his affair.

When I was at last free from St Cosimo's mercury baths,[35] I longed to be released from prison. I wrote to all my erstwhile friends urging them to do something to secure my freedom. My letters were never delivered, or perhaps their intended recipients just pretended not to have seen them. I was in despair and felt completely abandoned when I remembered the judge who deflowered me from behind. I implored him to intervene, and it was not in vain. Four days after I sent my request, I was free. Such were my feelings of gratitude that I would have offered him my maidenhead twenty times over and in the most bizarre postures, if he had asked.

Once released, I returned to society prettier than ever. The mineral baths that flowed through my veins renewed my health. I was ravishing, but still lacking something. Social graces and manners, I mean, and the invaluable secret of knowing how to enhance my natural gifts artfully. I naively believed that a clear complexion, fine features and a pretty face were enough. How ignorant was I of the ways of the world! Unaware of female wiles, I relied solely on my comely face to attract admirers. Far from being surrounded by followers, I was mortified to discover that any old crone with a wrinkled face caked with white powder and rouge had more luck than I. Since I did not want to return to *Bicêtre*, I submitted to becoming a painter's model to make ends meet.

During the six months I practised this profession, I had the honour of being an object both of study and of recreation for every dauber in Paris. There are few subjects sacred or profane that I have not modelled: from a penitent Mary Magdalene to Pasiphaë.[36] Today a saint, tomorrow a bawd, all according to what the artists wanted. Although I had one of the best figures in the business, a young laundress called Marguerite, but who now goes by the name of Mademoiselle Joly,[37] stole my thunder and all my clients. I was too well known, whereas Marguerite, who was no better looking than I, was fresh and new. They did not get as much out of her as they had hoped, however. Marguerite was such a bird-brain that she could not hold a pose. In order to paint her, you had to catch her on the wing, so to speak. Here's an example of how silly she was. One Monsieur T. was painting her as chaste Susannah,[38] in other words, without a stitch. He was obliged to leave the studio for a moment unexpectedly. In the meantime, a procession of Carmelite friars was passing in the street down below. Forgetting she was completely naked, Marguerite ran out on to the balcony to watch the procession. The townsfolk were more scandalized by her indecency than were the friars, and they greeted her with a hail of stones. The incident got Monsieur T. into hot water with the authorities who wanted to lynch him. In the end he got off by being excommunicated.

Marguerite's success with the painters meant that I had to look elsewhere. I took up with a Grey musketeer[39] who provided room and board and a hundred francs a month. I moved in, and we established a little nest in the rue du Chantre.[40] Monsieur de Mez (my benefactor) loved me with all his heart, and I loved him, which is odd since most kept women receive little more from their lover than a cold embrace. Be that as it may, I did not promise to be completely faithful. A young apprentice wig-maker and a broad-shouldered baker took turns behind my lover's back. The wig-maker took advantage of dressing my hair to come and go as he pleased. The baker, since he delivered bread to the house, acquired the same right without Monsieur de Mez suspecting a thing. Everything was perfect. My material needs were met, and I was still able to indulge in a few carnal delights. I had every reason to be pleased, and I was, when something unexpected upset the apple cart. The Court had retired to Fontainebleau.[41] Monsieur de Mez was on duty and confined to barracks. Our landlady, who knew my 'husband' was away from home, asked if she could let my room to a couple planning to spend a few nights in Paris. I agreed to give up my room and to share hers. The couple took possession of my bed that same night. They hoped to get a good night's sleep to make up for the fatigues of the road.

Monsieur de Mez, who was in the mood for love, arrived back in the house just as everyone had gone to bed. He had a pass key and a key for my room, which he entered quietly. What a shock he had when he heard a man's heavy snoring! He approached my bed trembling with jealous rage. He felt with his hands and found two heads on the pillows. Demon jealousy took over. He took his cane and started whacking blindly, striking the sleeping couple.[42] The husband received a broken arm trying to protect his wife. It's not hard to imagine that the din woke everyone in the house. The unfortunate couple's screams soon woke the neighbours. Everyone was running to and fro crying murder! Murder! The night watchman arrived just as Monsieur de Mez realized his mistake. He was arrested and taken to gaol. Since I was responsible for this fiasco, I thought it would be imprudent to wait and see what the outcome would be. I put on a skirt and petticoat and, during the ensuing confusion, I took refuge with a certain canon of St Nicholas, who happened to live under the same roof. He had had his eye on me for a long time. God knows, he was not displeased that the afore-described circumstances gave him the opportunity to satisfy his lecherous appetite. He received me with Christian charity and, after making me swallow a glass of sweetened brandy to lighten his conscience, he charitably introduced me into his canonical bed. It is not for nothing that the talents of these bead-mumblers are renowned. Compared to men of the cloth, men of the world are little better than pizzlewinks. The good father performed miracles of nature all night long, and then again until late the next day. Flaccid and worn out, it looked as if he might succumb to exhaustion, when suddenly his voluptuous imagination fired him off again. Every inch of my body was an object of worship, adoration and sacrifice. Neither Aretino[43] nor Clinchtel[§44] can have imagined as many poses as he did. Never were the mysteries of love celebrated with as much grace and in so many varied positions.

I became so close to that venerable canon that he offered to share with me his prebendary's stipend[45] which, in truth, amounted to very little. But I was in such dire straits that I could hardly turn my nose up at his offer.

That same evening, at the witching hour, he bade me put on a pair of drawers that for ten years had held his two prize jewels, an old filthy cassock as venerable as the drawers, a little lace-trimmed cloak and a collar. The devil himself would not have recognized me in this strange disguise. I looked less like a woman than one of those starving Irishmen who live from hand to mouth saying mass for a threepenny bit. You'll never guess where my new master was taking me. In the rue Champ-fleuri,[46] on the fifth floor, there lived an old hat hawker named Madame Thomas. This respectable lady was once the governess of our good canon. She left him to marry a neighbourhood water bearer who passed from this life to the next soon after the ceremony, leaving her nothing more than the riverbank fog. As a result of which situation, she enlisted as a companion in the venerable company of rag-sellers. As it turned out, the priest left me in the care of this elegant lady until such time as he could find me decent lodgings.

Madame Thomas was a fat, flat-nosed woman whose flesh hung loosely on her limbs. In spite of her excessive girth, one could see that she had once been pretty. The old girl maintained a secret commerce with a certain mendicant friar in the seraphic order of St Francis[47] who worshipped at her fleshy altar whenever libidinous feeling got the better of him.

The strange means by which fate effects miracles and leads mortals wherever she pleases are beyond human understanding. Could one have imagined that it would be in a hat-hawker's humble rooms that Lady Fortune would extend me a helping hand? Yet, nothing could be truer. Frère Alexis pulled me out of the gutter

---

[§] Painter famous for his obscenities.

and put me on the road that led to my present affluence. What defies human understanding is the way Fate will sometimes prepare the road to happiness by the most tragic events. A poor foreigner, who thinks himself perfectly safe, is pummelled in my room. He ends up with a broken arm. Afraid that I might be blamed, I hide with my neighbour who takes me to live with Madame Thomas. And that's not all. My holy guardian was killed, crushed and buried under the ruins of his own church.[§48] His sudden death left me without resource, at the mercy of my new hostess. The mere thought of the dire straits in which I found myself made me weep. Madame Thomas thought that the tears I shed were in memory of our recently departed friend. We cried together for a few moments. After which, the good lady, who was temperamentally opposed to lengthy shows of affliction, did her best to console me. She succeeded; her funny stories were better medicine than a theologian's claptrap.

— There, there missy, you'll just have to accept it, you will. Cry as we might till Judgement Day, it's just the way it is, in'it? Let God's will be done in all things, that's what I say. In the end, we didn't kill 'im, did we? It was 'is own fault, it was. What the devil did 'e have to go to matins for? He didn't go to matins more than four times a year. What a time to be pious! Ask me if they would not have been just as well without 'im singing. Ain't the cantor paid to sing? It's like Mère Michaud says, death comes like a thief in the night. It's when we least expect it that the Ol' Grim Reaper taps us on the shoulder. Who would 'ave thought to say yesterday to the late canon that we have a great fat goose for the morrow, we do, but you won't be gettin' any, not a bite. He would 'ave had none of that; no, indeed, 'e'd have sworn that 'e'd have his share, for, I declare, it's a goose worthy of a queen's table, it is. There, there, you see, let's be happy. All the grief in the world won't pay our debts. Besides, between you and me, 'e's not such a great loss. He cajoled the girls and promised, to tell the truth, more butter than bread. No, the funny bloke didn't mind sending them out to pasture once 'e'd had 'is fill. He made a god of 'is belly, 'e did; 'e drank and 'e owed money all over town. There, what's the point of hiding the truth now that 'e's dead? Upon my word 'e weren't worth three skips of a louse.

I was convinced by Madame Thomas's eulogy in honour of her late master that all servants are spies who censor our behaviour, dangerous because they have enough discernment to see our good qualities and invariably enough malice to spot our weakness and foibles. She spoke differently of Frère Alexis. True, his build won him many admirers among the fair sex. I mention this in passing since

[§] This tragedy actually happened fifteen or sixteen years ago. At the time several priests perished.

I satisfied my own curiosity regarding the Frère's prowess. Indeed, I often times have regretted that so much merit has been overlooked because of the monk's humble rags.

In order to avoid the criticism of not writing my tale in proper sequence, I ought to have first introduced this liveliest of monks at Madame Thomas's before mentioning his part in my story, as I have just done. I suppose it matters little. Never mind. Let us have him enter now that that good lady is busy stuffing the goose that she wants to feed him. I perceived a tall, well-built, vigorous and sinewy young cleric who wore a beard and whose fresh rosy complexion shone brightly under a penetrating fiery gaze that stirred something below the heart, giving me an itch my fingers could not relieve.

Madame Thomas told him all about me. By the bye, he learned the sad tale of the canon. He consoled himself just as we did, as all reasonable people do when misfortune cannot be remedied. The fellow did not limit his activities to those of a mendicant friar. He found a secret way to be useful to society, and even more so to his convent, through services rendered to both sexes. No one knew better than he how to pull off an amorous intrigue, how to lift obstacles, how to elude a father's watchful eye, how to trick jealous husbands, how to emancipate young maidens from parental tyranny. In a word, Frère Alexis was the king of procurers,[49] and for that reason he was highly acclaimed among people of fashion.

After the introductions, Madame Thomas went out of doors in order to put her goose in the oven.[50] She no sooner had gone downstairs than the monk, without so much as a by-your-leave, planted a kiss on my mouth and then pushed me on the bed.

Although I found this behaviour alarming and strange, the need I might have of his services, coupled with the desire to see for myself what lay hidden under his cassock, made me feign resistance enough to inflame his passions and to avoid his taking me for a common streetwalker.

Once he got me into position, he lifted his skirts up over his thighs and proceeded to yank out of his heavy leather drawers the most beautiful, the most superb symbol of manhood, an ivory sceptre worthy of a royal codpiece rather than the grubby loincloth of a soldier in the army of St Francis. Ah! Madame Thomas, how many women would gladly trade places with you? The Queen of love herself, the adorable Venus, would have given up Mars and Adonis for the pleasure of a precious thumper like that. Priapus and all his minions penetrated my body. The sharp pain that that venerable rod gave ought to have made me scream aloud, but I was afraid to frighten the neighbours. The initial pain, however, soon gave way to the most delicious suffering. How can I describe the enchanting, melting fits of pleasure, the thrilling moments when I thought I should faint … the sweet ecstasy … Ah! The imagination is powerless to express our deepest feelings. This is hardly surprising since in those delectable moments the soul is annihilated and we exist only through the senses.

I would have suffocated with delight had we not been interrupted by the sound of Madame Thomas's loud voice scolding her dog in the stairway. She must have known what was going on; the state we were in and the disorderly bed-clothes were squarely against us. Still, she said nothing about it. When the goose arrived we tucked in, smacking our lips and raising many a bumper. Between cheese and pudding, Frère Alexis pulled out of his satchel a Bologna sausage and a bottle of sweet brandy given him by some fancy ladies who had spent the night carousing in Neuilly.[51] Madame Thomas had a fondness for this liquor, and she drank half the bottle. She was in such good spirits that she rolled her eyes like a she-cat in heat lusting after her tom. Watching her squirm in her chair, you would have sworn that she had nettles in her drawers. That must have been where the brandy was fermenting, for she was suddenly given to fits of both violence and sweetness. She kissed the monk, then pinched him, then sucked at his face, bit him and tickled him. In the end I felt sorry for her. I withdrew to a small closet whose walls were little more than a partition with gaps an inch wide, papered over. Cutting a small hole in the paper, I had a front row seat and could watch their manoeuvres unobserved.

The attentive reader will recall that I described Madame Thomas as a jolly tub of lard and therefore will not be shocked when I explain the pose she struck for Frère Alexis. The good lady had such a fearsome belly that it would have been well-nigh impossible to take her from the front. In truth, a Mirebalay[§] donkey could not have done the job. She consequently put her elbows on the bed and her pug nose on the coverlet, and then raised her immense posteriors high enough to reach Frère Alexis. In an instant the lecher threw her petticoat and shift over her shoulders, revealing her rounded buttocks which, in spite of their prodigious volume, were still a fair sight owing to their excessive whiteness. Alexis, lifting his skirts, took hold of the seraphic aspergillum[52] he had just sprinkled me with and proceeded with inexpressible vigour into the thicket located between the above mentioned buttocks, losing himself, so to speak, in the bushes.

In the heat of the action, Madame Thomas shrieked and cursed like a she-devil. The excess of pleasure left her raging as if she were in intolerable pain. But from time to time the tone of her ejaculations softened. 'Stop you're killing me,' she cried, her voice quivering with sighs.

— My pet, how I love you. Hang on, hang on my pet, my precious gem… Ah! Son of a whore! Bugger! Stop! In the name of God, you're killing me! Ah! Are you never going to stop? My pet, forgive me, forgive me! Save me! I can take it no longer.

I confess that I did not have the strength to watch that lustful scene coldly. I sought some relief in the use of my fingers, when suddenly I saw a bit of candle

---

§ Village in Brittany famous for its donkeys.

on a shelf. I grabbed it and shoved it in as far as it would go, my eyes fixed on the two performers I was watching. I was unable to quench the fire in my soul, but at least I could contain it.

One ought not to be surprised that Madame Thomas had so little modesty and that she performed this scene aware that I would hear it and almost certainly suspecting that I would watch. First, she was in no state to give any thought to social graces, but even if she had been, she was under no obligation to me since she was fully aware of my profession. She either wanted to give proof of her full confidence and friendship, or, rather more likely, she got it in her head to watch a scene just like the one I had observed. Thus she removed Frère Alexis's underpants and put his still smoking prick in my hand. Had I the inclination to play the coy one, I scarcely had the time. The lusty friar pushed me on the bed and quickly made a mask of my shift. His redoubtable torch missed its intended mark and, entering, gave me such cramps that I thought my belly should burst. Charitable Madame Thomas, touched by my sufferings, came to the rescue and redirected the tenon to its proper mortise.[53] I was in no position to thank her for her help, but I reckoned that my furiously thrusting hips would leave her in no doubt as to the extent of my gratitude.

The friar, unshakable in the saddle, responded to my bucking with sharp energetic jerks that, on any other occasion, would have made me fear that the floor was about to collapse. Lust, however, made me fearless. Were the house on fire, I should not have been bothered, proving that there are occasions when women are capable of great courage. Still, I cannot remember ever being so determined to take my pleasure. Only a champion like Frère Alexis could manage my frenzy. I was a demon. I wrapped my legs around his calves and squeezed the small of his back with both arms so that nothing could make me let go. The honour of having subdued me was his alone. What was truly incredible was that, without taking time to catch his breath, he thrice put me in seventh heaven. O proud gentlemen and ladies of fashion, when will you recognize your own weakness and the red-blooded prowess of the cloth?

On the basis of this tryst, Frère Alexis got it in his head that I was a talented young wench. He assured me, in a prophet's voice, that I could make a fortune.

— I could easily find you a gallant suitor, but that would not get you anywhere. Your face and your figure are enough to raise you above a situation as mediocre as that. Now that I think about it, the Opera[54] is your calling. I shall do my best to get you a foot in the door. The question is whether you can sing or dance.

— I think I will have more luck dancing.

— I think so too, he said, uncovering my leg above the knee. Now there's something made for dancing. Upon my word, all the opera glasses will be on you.

Frère Alexis did not make promises without following through. Presently, he gave me a letter of recommendation for Monsieur de Gr — M —, in those days gatekeeper of that stable of fillies known as the Opera. The very next day, Madame Thomas having found me some second-hand clothes, I dressed as best I could; around noon I delivered my epistle to its address.

I met a tall, withered, dark and stolid man whose chilly manner was enough to make you catch cold. He was wearing an open dressing-gown without underclothes; when a draught parted his shirt tails, one could plainly see two large white rough thighs between which dangled the sad, shrivelled wreckage of his virility.

I noted that while he read the letter he looked me over attentively and that his austere expression softened. It occurred to me that this was a good omen. I was not mistaken. Monsieur Gr — M — sat me down beside him and told me that my pretty face and figure were recommendation enough, but that, nevertheless, he welcomed with joy the opportunity to court the public by presenting a specimen like me.

While he was making these flattering remarks, he took inventory of my most intimate charms. Little by little, lust was aroused in the old rake's heart. He bade me put my hand on his deplorable relic of a prick. I needed all the lessons learned at Madame Florence's school to restore that shapeless mass to vigour, to rescue it, in other words, from its present feeble state. At first his flesh was insensitive. It stubbornly resisted my repeated stroking and my rubbing his jewels. I began to despair at the success of my efforts when presently it occurred to me to stroke his perineum and to 'socratise'[55] him with the tip of my finger. This expedient worked wonders. The tired old wreck rose slowly from its lethargy. It expanded and grew to such an extent that it took on an entirely new being. In order to take advantage of this precious moment, I wriggled my wrist so quickly and smoothly that the monster, overcome with the most delirious sensations, shed a torrent of pearly tears.

At length Monsieur de Gr — M —, won over by my good manners, dressed and took me straight away to Monsieur Thuret,[56] at that time director of the Opera. I was fortunate enough that he too fancied me. Without hesitation, he admitted me to the glittering corps of the Royal Academy of Music[§] and then asked us to luncheon.

I like to vary my portraits and the scenes I describe, so I shall say nothing about what took place between Monsieur Thuret and me. Suffice it to say that the good man was every bit as lecherous as Monsieur Gr — M — and not less difficult to get up and running. Meanwhile, I was anxious to tell Madame Thomas the outcome of Frère Alexis's letter, and so I went to her rooms to sleep.

[§] The Opera House.

The next day I returned to my former lodgings, no longer concerned about the police.

Apart from the lessons backstage,§ which I never missed, Malterre le Diable[57] gave me private tuition. I made such rapid progress that in less than three months I could stand on both legs tolerably well in the ballet.

My début was marked by an amusing incident. One of our associates was found in a state of mortal sin backstage. The female conclave no sooner learned of this episode than an exemplary punishment was demanded. The delinquent was brought before Monsieur Thuret to be judged. Inspector Madame La Camarée might have been inclined to issue a pardon, but Madame Justice Cartou and her assistants Mesdames Fanchon Chopine, Desaigles and Mother Carville declared how dangerous it was to pardon such crimes, that new girls made bold by the example of unpunished, villainous debauchery would soon fall into the excesses displayed by the girls at the *Opéra Comique*.[58] Madame Justice Cartou added that it would be a source of shame, nay, of infamy, to allow prostitution of this type to be associated with a theatre that had always been a school of chivalrous behaviour of the most refined and distinguished kind. Lastly, that unless the guilty party were severely reprimanded, no honest girl would want her name associated with the Opera. Thus, Fanchon Chopine wrapped up the prosecution demanding that the poor child's name be struck from the company. The others nodded in agreement. Seeing that arguing would serve no useful purpose, Monsieur Thuret stripped the guilty party of her honours and prerogatives and deprived her forthwith of the right of showing her Chinese face on stage.

I had been loafing around with the students of Terpiscore§ for about a week when one morning I received a billet-doux which read like this:

Mademoiselle, I saw you yesterday at the Opera. Your face seduced me. I think you can come to an agreement with a man who abhors awkwardness in his love life and who does not dare utter a sigh without a fistful of gold to back it up. Please send word to me at once.

I am etc.

Although I did not have enough experience of the world to know a man by his epistolary style, I guessed with little difficulty, by the concise aridity of this note, that I had touched the heart of a financier. When they come along, friends like that are too precious to pass over. I didn't play stupid. I answered on the spot that I was greatly honoured that he singled me out among so many lovely girls at the Opera and that it would be unworthy of his kindness to refuse his offer of support

§ Storage area where scenery is kept and where the company rehearses.
§ Muse of the Dance.

and finally, that if he were impatient to meet, I was just as impatient to assure him personally of my profound respect.

An hour after I had responded to his letter there arrived at my door a beautifully appointed horse and carriage which, without being excessively ostentatious, confirmed the wealth of its owner. I greeted him with appropriate formality in the courtyard. To describe him in three words: he was a short stocky man, frightfully ugly, about sixty years of age. He mumbled about five or six gallant phrases which I would never have understood had he not slipped into my hand a roll of fifty *louis d'or*. Any conversation, however dull, is fascinating, and even sublime, when supplemented by generosity. Not only did what he have to say suddenly seem ingenuously expressed, I presently thought I could perceive in his features a certain air of distinction, of nobility, that I had not picked up on at first glance. Such is the rationale of good manners; one cannot help but be found attractive when one starts off on the right foot.

I was wearing a thin déshabillé, in truth more revealing than stylish. The art with which I wore it was so closely allied to nature herself that my charms appeared to owe nothing to my raiment. I had every reason to rely on their intoxicating power. My financier found me adorable. The hunger in his eyes convinced me that the little scene we were playing would soon draw to its inevitable conclusion. Yet, after three quarters of an hour of merry banter, I was dropped like the proverbial hot potato. This humiliation was especially mortifying as I had never before been fobbed off in quite that way. I was terrified that he had found some imperfection in my appearance that had escaped my eye. Happily, he reassured me that he was often subject to lose interest at the last minute. He was speaking the truth. During the year that we were together, the same thing happened on a regular basis at least twice a week. Be that as it may, many girls would have been quite contented to find themselves kept under such easy terms. He furnished a set of rooms for me in the rue Sainte-Anne;[59] he paid for my lodging and provided, on top of that, ten *louis d'or* a month. I was sitting on a gold mine when his situation suddenly changed for the worse, putting an end to our liaison.

Everything at the Opera depends on acquiring the right reputation. Nothing adds to an actress's glamour more than being the cause of a couple of spectacular bankruptcies, or sending one's lovers to the hospital. The ruin of my financier established my reputation once and for all. A crowd of suitors closed in on me. I did not like to choose one over the other without seeking the advice of Monsieur de Gr — M — and Frère Alexis, with whom I felt a special bond. Allow me to add, by way of a memorandum, the sound advice I received from these two men as a testimony of my gratitude toward them, and as a guide for girls who want to live off their charms.

Advice for a young lady of the world

Item:

- Any woman who wishes to achieve her ends must emulate the merchant and set her sights on her own interest and profits.
- Her heart must be closed to true love. It is enough that she act as if she were in love and that she know how to make others fall in love with her.
- He who pays best wins out over his rivals.
- She must have as little as possible to do with men of quality. Most are haughty and dishonest. Big financiers are more dependable and easier to manage. The trick is how to catch them.
- If she is wise, she will avoid the company of young bucks and men of fashion; besides bringing in little money, they frighten off those who do.
- When a worthwhile punter comes along, she must not worry about being unfaithful; such is the price of the trade.
- Insofar as it is possible, she should imitate Mademoiselle Durocher,[§60] who would only indulge in delicacies when she didn't have to pay for them.
- She should invest her money as it comes in and get a good return on her investment.
- If a foreign gentleman and a Frenchman of similar wealth find themselves in competition for her favours, she must decide in favour of the former. Besides being a requirement of common courtesy, she will get more satisfaction from the foreigner, especially if he be a Lord from the City of London.[§] Although real dunderheads, these gentlemen are so proud that they are capable of losing their shirt in order to make us believe that they are richer than they are.
- She will take care of her health and avoid intimacy with Americans, Spaniards and Neapolitans, taking into account that: *Timeo danaos et dons ferentes.*[§61]
- Finally, she must suppress her own personality and study that of her lover in order to take on his character as if it were her own.

Signed: Gr — M — and Frère Alexis

May all girls in the trade commit this treatise to memory and make use of it as well as I have.

[§] Formerly mistress of Lord Weymouth.

[§] Banking and business district.

[§] Let us remember that Margot grew up in the street; she must therefore know many different sorts of language.

The first chump who replaced my financier was a baron, son of a big Hamburg merchant. I do not think that Germany ever produced a sillier, more disagreeable blockhead. He was over six feet tall, red-headed, knock-kneed, extremely stupid, and an incorrigible drunk. This young gentleman — hope and idol of his adoring parents — was living abroad to complete his education and to supplement his native habits with the refinements one acquires in good company. The only decent house he frequented in Paris was his banker's, who was under strict orders to dole out all the money he required. His friends consisted of a couple of easy-going scroungers and several buffoons who hung about Madame Lacroix's[§] harem.

Monsieur Gr — M —, always thinking of my best interests, was of the view that it would be a great loss if a young pigeon like the baron escaped our dovecote. He gave the baron to understand that a gentleman of his breeding ought to cut a certain figure in the world and that nothing could contribute to his becoming a man of fashion better than his being seen about the town with a pretty actress on his arm. It is in just such company that all the young noblemen, as well as our first-class magistrates, acquire their fine manners and fashionable tone.

The baron, open to this advice, confided that he had long had a love interest at the Opera, and that love interest was me.

— Dammy, replied Monsieur G — M —, your taste is first rate, you know. One would swear you've been a fine swell for a decade or more. D'you know, so far as anyone can recall, there has never been a more exquisite creature on the Parisian stage. She's been as free as a bird now for just over a month, and I'm told the poor creature is harassed on all sides, knowing not whom to choose. Leave it with me. I'll work something out for you. It's not in the bag. No sir, but what makes me hopeful is that she has a staggering weakness for foreign gentlemen. I must tell you, though, that she's not just out for the money. Oh no, she's a *gel* who could really fall for the right man. Do you hear what I'm saying? A gentleman in a position to treat her as she deserves to be treated. You would not believe how attached she was to her last beau. Mind you, he was worthy of her. Never, no never has a gentleman behaved with more decorum towards a mistress, so noble, so distinguished. Naturally, she tried to hide from him her occasional pecuniary needs (in truth what pretty *gel* does not need money?). Oh, but he could see right through her little games. Yes! I always said their love was one constant struggle: her indifference to money at odds with his touching generosity.

The baron, fascinated by Monsieur Gr — M —'s rapturous praise, begged him to employ his best efforts to bring about a rendezvous, whatever the cost.

[§] Madame as renowned as Madame Florence or Madame Paris.

In order to whet his appetite, I resolved not to rush into anything and to let several days pass before agreeing to his demands. Our first meeting took place at the Opera during a rehearsal of *Jephté*,[62] on which occasion he had the pleasure of respectfully kissing my hand in the wings. I was not displeased that our first meeting should take place during a rehearsal, for ordinarily, it is in this very context that the ladies of the stage appear in all their pride and pomp, and that they vie with one another to show off both the extravagance and the vulnerability of their fatuous lovers.

Although I had thus far caused the downfall of only one man, I already had sufficient jewels and finery to hold my own amongst the first ladies of the Opera. I could therefore take my place, like them, sitting on a chair[§] beside the orchestra, one leg nonchalantly resting on my knee. It was chilly that afternoon. Never had anyone appeared in a more sumptuous, more imposing déshabillé. Softly wrapped in ermine and sable, my feet were hidden in a crimson velvet box lined with bear-skin, in which a hot water bottle had been placed to keep me warm. In this ostentatious get-up, I distractedly played with my ribbons, making little bows with a golden shuttle. From time to time, I looked at my watch, made it ring; I rattled my snuff-boxes and opened them one after the other and then sniffed at a precious rock crystal flask to alleviate vapours I had not. Leaning over to whisper little nothings to my colleagues, I gave the assembled onlookers ample opportunity to size up my well-turned limbs. In a word, I behaved with exquisite insolence entirely for the enchantment of our half-witted spectators. The men who met my eyes gave me a deep bow full of respect and considered themselves fortunate if I responded with an imperceptible nod.

In moments of triumph like the one I have just described, it was not possible for me to give more than a passing thought to my humble origins. The luxury to which I had grown accustomed combined with the grovelling of the gentlemen who vied for my favours, obliterated the memory of my former life. I thought myself a goddess. How could I not, exalted as I was by the blind worship of men of the highest rank? Frankly it is men, and not us, who are to blame for our insolence and our affected airs. It is they who turn our heads with their flattery and their blandishments. How can we be blamed for getting carried away with ourselves when, in truth, we take our cue from our gentlemen admirers? Forgive me ladies, dear friends, for expressing myself so boldly on your behalf. My frankness in no wise harms your interests. Even if I wanted to, I could not. For as long as there are men in the world, there will be fools enough for you.

Returning to my baron, I soon perceived that my sweetness had roused in him a kind of ecstatic rapture, and that he was no longer a free man. From the start of the rehearsal, his large eyes watched me like those of an English pointer; he

---

[§] Distinction reserved for kept women.

seemed in the thrall of tortures akin to those of a holy martyr. I paid him the honour, once the rehearsal was over, of accepting a place in his coach and then inviting him to supper. Monsieur Gr — M —, who stayed behind to tend to the affairs of the company, joined us half an hour later. I did not want to destroy the excellent image of me that he had given the baron, and so I behaved on that occasion with utmost dignity, playing the part of the sentimental girl to such perfection that the poor fool thought I was capable of sincere infatuation.

Nature compensates fools by giving them a double dose of pride. The more ridiculous and unpleasant they are, the more endowed with merit they believe themselves to be. Such was the baron's weakness. He was convinced that I was in love with him as much as he was in love with me. I naturally fuelled this flattering assumption by pampering him at supper. When he took his leave, I said, looking with an expression full of longing, that I would expect him the next day at my house for chocolate. (I planned on this occasion to test his generosity.) He was so punctual that I was still in bed when his arrival was announced. I quickly donned a peignoir and, unlike most girls, I had nothing to fear by showing myself without first having artfully arranged my appearance. Thus I received him in a negligee with all the pouting and platitudes customary under the circumstances.

— How *fery charmink*, he said, to catch someone in bed at *zis* hour.
— Goodness, what time can it be? Your watch must be running fast. Oh gracious! Look at me. I look a fright, ghastly, perfectly ghastly. I am horrified to be seen in this state. Do you know, I did not sleep a wink all night. At this very moment I have a splitting headache. No matter. The pleasure of seeing you will make it go away. Lisette, let's have some chocolate, and remember that I like it thick.

My orders were executed in a flash. While we were regaling our noses and palates with the creamy drink, I was informed that my jeweller was at the door asking leave to see me.

— Ah! Such interruptions! Didn't I tell you that I'm not at home for anyone? Servants are an odd lot. You can talk to them until you are blue in the face; they do exactly as they please. It makes me so angry. With your permission, perhaps, I should find out what he wants. Tell him to come in... Hello, my dear Monsieur de La Frenaie.[63] What brings you to this part of town so early? How is business? I suppose you have some new trinket to show me.
— Madame,[§] that's precisely what induced me to take the liberty of calling. I thought you would not be displeased to have a look at a *croix à la devote*[64]

[§] In order to avoid any misunderstanding, whores call themselves 'Madame'.

that a financier's wife, who lives in the *Place Vendôme*,[65] ordered from me. I can say without the slightest pretension that an object of this quality does not happen my way every day.

— Monsieur de La Frenaie, you are too kind to think of your friends; I am gratified by this mark of consideration. Well, let's have a look, since you're so obliging. Ah, my dear baron, isn't it beautiful? The setting is exquisite, marvellous. The stones are superb, beautifully cut. Don't you find they sparkle admirably? Nowadays, it is the insolent wives of bankers who wear the most sumptuous jewels. For my part, I can only regret that such a gorgeous jewel is set aside for a woman of that ilk. If you don't mind my asking, how much do you want for it?

— Madame, eight thousand francs is the best I can do.

— If I had ready money, I would not suffer you to take it away.

— You know, Madame, that everything that is mine is at your disposal. If the fancy takes you …

— Oh no, I never buy anything on credit.

The baron, as I had surmised, was delighted to have such a perfect opportunity to woo me. He grasped the cross and immediately paid sixty *tournoi*[66] down, with a promissory note to settle the balance the following day. I naturally played the indignant female whose motives are as noble as they are disinterested.

— I declare, sir, you're not being reasonable. You've gone beyond being generous. I am telling the truth. I am not in the least pleased. Admittedly, it's not a crime to accept some trifle from a gentleman one thinks highly of, for whom one feels some inclination. But, honestly, you've gone too far. I could never allow myself to accept it.

During this rant, the cretin fastened the cross around my neck. Then I got up and absentmindedly went into my bedchamber. He followed me. Without making him languish any longer, I proceeded to give him at the foot of the bed adequate compensation for his eight thousand francs. I played the scene with such convincing sincerity that he thought my feelings were inspired by his personal qualities and not by the gift I had just received.

Monsieur de Gr — M —, to whom I had confided beforehand my intention to bleed the baron dry, joined us at luncheon. His well-earned commission was a gold snuff-box *à la Maubois*.[67] Since there was no performance that afternoon, we dined in, all three. Each had good reason to be satisfied with the deal struck. Consequently, our merrymaking was all light-heartedness. The baron was in especially fine form. Having gabbled a lot of clumsy German jokes, and much the worse for drink, he soon lost what little good sense he had. We sent him packing dead drunk.

After this test of his munificence, I conceived that the way to get the best of him was to avoid a set arrangement, whilst continuing to play the part of the infatuated lover. This strategy succeeded beyond my wildest dreams. In less than a month I took delivery of a complete service of silver. Although it is true that a devotee's lavish gifts are more liable to inspire contempt than love, I was surprised, after affecting so many pouting scowls, to find myself very nearly in love.

Habit grows on one and makes one adapt to the flaws in those whose company we keep. As sullen and stupid as he was, I began to find the baron less unpleasant than I had initially, when an unforgivable *faux pas* on his part confirmed my erstwhile feelings of contempt. He was much given to drink and unfortunately, he never felt more amorous than when drunk. One evening, after a day of feasting and drinking in the most disreputable company, he presented himself at the very moment I was getting ready for bed. The great hulk tripped on the threshold, lost his balance and fell face down on the floor. The fall was not light given his state. When we got him on his feet, he was covered in blood and nearly comatose. If I'd had time to faint I would have done so, but the urgency of the situation required immediate action. I flew to my dressing closet and returned with four flasks of different spirits. I thought he was more seriously injured than subsequently proved to be the case, so I set about washing his face repeatedly. I made him swallow a teaspoon of *arquebuse* water.[68] The swine had barely a taste of it on his lips when he was seized with a violent fit of hiccups. In the same moment, he spewed half his supper in my face. I can scarcely describe the horrible scene that followed. I retched so hard that I almost choked on my own blood. I stripped off my nightclothes and had to spend more than four *louis d'or* on scent and mouthwash to rid myself of the stench.

In this angry state, I had him thrown out and made sure that his man-servant understood that he was never to set foot on the premises again. The next morning, he learned what had taken place the night before and was consequently in a state of desperation. He wrote me several letters that I returned unopened. As a last resort, he appealed to Monsieur de Gr — M — for help. He fell headlong into the trap. Far from calming the baron's worries, that crafty old fox exaggerated the gravity of his infraction. The poor baron was overcome with guilt. He cried, moaned and bellowed and got so carried away that Monsieur de Gr — M — grew frightened that he would hang himself and that we would be held accountable for it. He then changed tack.

— You're talking about the most generous *gel* in the world, he said in a plummy voice. And so much the better for you! Horrible though your offence may be, I would not give up hope that with an appropriate expression of remorse and submissiveness, you might just win her back. I believe this to be the case, for I know without doubt that she's simply mad about you. She may hide her true feelings behind a mask of pride, but her inclination nevertheless betrays itself in spite of her best efforts to hide it. Only yesterday, but please keep this under your hat, I really shouldn't say. Oh well, only yesterday, her eyes welled up with tears when I mentioned your name. She confessed that no gentleman ever inspired the feelings in her that you have. One thing is for sure, the poor child has not slept a wink since your little tiff. And bad luck never strikes once. She has had to deal with a scoundrel of an upholsterer who is forcing her to sell all her furniture in order to settle a measly debt of 2000 *écus*.

— *Vivat*! cried the baron, taking him in his arms. You *haff* just *profided* me, *vithout knowink* what you were saying, with the most *charmink* opportunity to make a peace *offerink*. *Zat* money-grubbing scamp *vill* be paid off tomorrow, or there's not a penny in Paris.

— My good fellow, that's what I call a triumph of wit. The idea, although completely obvious, would never have occurred to me in a hundred years. But now that you mention it, the gesture is indeed worthy of a nobleman of your high standing, and of the charming *gel* whose distress it is intended to alleviate. Yes, yes, I am of your view. You could not come up with a better way to overcome her bitterness. Her heart is far too soft not to be deeply touched by such a noble gesture. You must, however, hurry to put the money together and then come and fetch me. I'll take care of the rest.

The fool acted with such diligence that within the space of twenty-four hours Gr — M — brought him to me with 250 shining *louis d'or* in hand. Their harmonious clinking brought tears to my eyes. Seeing me weep touched him to the point that he began to bawl like a calf, the result being that our reconciliation was ludicrously touching. Only a man as phlegmatic as Gr — M — could maintain a serious expression in the face of such a preposterous scene. Following our reconciliation, the love and generosity of the baron reached such a pitch that I would have bled him dry had his worthy father, having learned of his son's profligacy, not presented himself in person and ordered his son back home. Thus finished my story with the Adonis from Holstein.

Enticed by the large sums I had just raised in enemy territory, I made up my mind to concentrate on foreign affairs and to force the hand of luck, having already decided that I had no desire to grow old in the trade. According to my plan, two or three blockheads like the last one, and I would be in clover, so to speak, for the rest of my career. But such good fortune cannot be taken for granted. I made up my mind to take things in hand and decided, for the time being, to launch an offensive on home turf in the hopes that another baron would turn up.

It is the custom for courtesans who have recently been abandoned by their amoroso to appear in public frequently, thus alerting prospective gentlemen friends that they are available. In accordance with this time-worn custom, I put in an appearance at all the best places, with the exception of the *Tuileries*, where, since that mortifying incident involving Mademoiselle Durocher, we are no longer permitted to show our faces.[§][69]

The *Palais-Royal*[70] is the perfect enclave. Our right to appear there is unchallenged, having been secured many years ago, the Opera being situated nearby. Here, in this garden of indulgence, we are free to strut and act the part of women of condition: in a word, to confront the onlooker, flaunting our elegant airs and pride. Certain outspoken detractors protest in vain that only money-lenders, young bucks and strumpets haunt the *Palais-Royal*. Neither their jealousy nor their hateful insinuations stop the idle youth of Paris, magistrates, fashionable red-coats and young clergymen, from gathering there, especially in the evening before a performance at the Opera. A throng of beautiful women of every description constitutes the chief attraction. The flowery banks they form, arranged on seats under the trees, offer the eye a charming spectacle, at once glorious and gracious, and whose admirable variety defies description. A thousand tender sighs, transformed into as many fluttering sparrows, give the place its own unique air of reckless abandon. Why should that be surprising? If it is true that the whore is the very soul of pleasure, that pleasure follows her everywhere, it follows that the places over which she presides must be the most agreeable in the world. No?

To be sure, our miraculous ability to charm enlivens all manner of company in every setting. Gallantry, nay prurience, accompany us wherever we go, and even unto places of worship. Take, for example, the chapel of the *Quinze-Vingts*[71] where we have special privileges and are consequently permitted to flaunt our wares in much the same way as we do in the *Palais-Royal* or at the theatre. Lord knows how many pious souls gather there on Sundays or on feast days just to see us at prayer. Their prying glances and low bows literally besiege us. What's more … they hum popular ditties in our ears during the mass. We respond to these touching signs of affection with ribaldry and laughter, half hiding our faces behind our fans. Communion over, without our so much as being aware of the priest's slowness, indeed, without our even having noticed if he was at the altar, the inevitable conclusion of our devotions was a supper party planned for some house or other, or better still, an assignation with a prospective punter.

One day, I struck such a deal and was taken advantage of in a most humiliating way. One of those *chevaliers*, who has nothing in this world save his own gallant charm, and who, owing to the unpardonable negligence of the chief of police, makes his living blackmailing and plundering the honest townsfolk; one of these rascals, whose air of superiority and free spending inspire awe, found the means

[§] She was almost tossed in a fountain for having the effrontery to make an ostentatious display of her wealth in the presence of a royal princess.

to get himself included in all our little entertainments. A picnic in the *bois de Boulogne*,[72] a supper at the *Glacière*,[73] would have been unthinkable without his being invited.

Allow me to observe by way of a short digression that frequenting gentlemen of this sort is fraught with risk. Most have a sweet, insinuating and sociable nature, and beautiful engaging manners. In a word, they are consummate masters of the social graces. I will add that experience has taught me to be on my guard when confronted by those who are overly polite. They are almost never true gentlemen.

Back to the story of my con-artist. I had long hankered for the superb diamond ring that he sported. The double-dealer often said that it would be a small price to pay for certain trifling favours. I pretended to pay no mind. I nonetheless thought too highly of my pretty face to think he spoke only in jest. I was convinced that sooner or later I would have the ring for myself.

I thought the occasion was ripe on Sunday. I was at mass at the *Quinze-Vingts*. The *chevalier* joined me and proceeded with eloquence and sweetness to pitch his wooing. I responded that I would have every reason to be delighted with his pretty phrases if I could only persuade myself that they were sincere.

— Ah! he cried out, uttering a sigh worthy of an actor. Do you have eyes and discernment enough to see only merit in others and never in yourself?
— Let us suppose I have some merit, I responded coolly, and that I ignore not the fact. Am I still not justified in questioning a gentleman's lovemaking? Are men not frequently unfaithful? Do they not deceive women every day? Women who have more merit than I? Ah! Monsieur le chevalier, I am afraid that if one asked for some assurance that your feelings are true, you would be sorely disconcerted.
— What? Do you think me a rogue?
— I want to believe you, I interrupted, just as I would like to believe all the others who say three quarters of the time what they think not, and who often make promises they do not keep. Admit, for example — unless the offer was only in jest — that you would have been knocked for six if I had taken you at your word when you offered me your diamond ring.
— Madame, he responded with some pique, before passing judgement on others, you ought to put them to the test.
— Prithee sir, what would you have me do? I said smiling. As a general rule, the good suffers in the place of the bad. Men are so false that it is not a great injustice to have a low opinion of you and your kind. But since I have no reason to judge you personally too rigorously, I can make an exception in your favour, and believe that you have in common with your sex only those qualities that are a credit to it. Surely, it is not fitting to reflect on such matters in company. Come to me for a quiet lunch. We can talk more comfortably.

Thus, I fell into his trap. The first thing he did was to put his ring on my finger. The rapture that I felt in possession of such a magnificent jewel meant that I was in no position to refuse to satisfy his pressing desire. Before and after our little meal, I gave him as many expressions of gratitude as his heart could wish for. Now, will you believe what this little lesson cost me? The diamond was paste. A gold snuff-box went missing. The villain made off with it. I had no other profit than that for which the gentlemen doctors of St Cosimo prescribe a draft of cooling diuretics. The upsetting part of this sad business is that, far from being able to get my own back, or for that matter, far from even being able to grumble quietly about the dirty trick he played on me, I trembled lest he make it public. In a word, I was so concerned that he would talk that, had he threatened to do so, I might well have consented to pay him to keep quiet. I was prudent enough, however, to swallow the pill quietly and go on a light diet without saying a word. To help the medicine do its work quickly, I claimed to have a chest complaint. Monsieur Thuret excused me from dancing. I nevertheless did not miss a performance at the Opera, arriving *incognito* in the amphitheatre, unkempt in appearance and with my hair combed forward. Good Lord, what a lot of rot I could repeat if I wrote down all the tiresome small talk I heard on all sides. A swarm of chatterboxes buzzed in my ears. How can men be at once so empty-headed and so pernickety? Is it possible that women are so hard-up for compliments and base adulation that they are taken in by, nay, that they take pleasure in such idiotic remarks?

In the middle of all these dull men, there was a certain pale financier, a staggering hulk in truth, who lisped with impressive confidence the most absurd flattery ever uttered by an imbecile. Then there was an old toothless grey-beard, a real sweet-talker capable of making one nod off with boredom, but who, nevertheless, outdid himself trying to inspire a passion in my breast for his wrinkled little eyes with a repertoire of dulcet phrases lifted from the *roman d'Astrée*.[74] Some distance from these two imposing gentlemen, a group of smug young men kept casting discreet, passionate glances my way. They muttered under their breath, but loud enough to turn my head, that I was charming, a real beauty, prettier than an angel, brighter than the stars. When I looked their way, they modestly lowered their gaze, in order to convince me that since the compliments they paid my charms were not intended for my ears, they could not be accused of vile flattery.

When I think of so much impudence, I am almost convinced that women of my type have an intoxicating power of attraction, and that men are blind. The rage in France for the kept woman is so great that men are genuinely more gratified to entertain a liaison with an actress than with the most distinguished ladies of the realm, be their distinction one of birth or of personal merit. Can it not all be put down to the futile need to be talked about? I maintain that it is we who give our lovers their sense of worth. A man lost in the crowd, an insignificant fellow, suddenly sports the title of man of fashion once he is seen to keep a mistress.

How many crass business types make a name for themselves by having their fortune plundered by some bird? It is the courtesan who, by her exorbitant demands, draws the otherwise clumsy bourgeois out of obscurity and puts his name in the public eye. Is it not to Mademoiselle Pellicier that Ulysses owes his renown?[75] For renown, you must agree, comes in many forms. It is without doubt that incomparable siren who enhanced the lady of pleasure's reputation, thanks, in part, to her adventures with that infamous Jew. Thanks, that is to say, to the theft of his diamonds and the subsequent adventures she was mixed up in, his name is consecrated for all time, not only as a man once fantastically rich, but also as one who died penniless. Such is the glorious advantage of being caught in our nets. A man may lose face and a good deal of money. His compensation is the great figure he cuts in the fashionable world, and the reputation he acquires by being talked about.

Let us return, however, to my own story. For three weeks, I had been cooling my blood with an herbal infusion of strawberry-plant roots, water lily and saltpetre, when a woman dealing in old clothes proposed, to tide me over, a liaison with a deputy of the clergy. I was feeling much more like myself but was unsure that I was completely cured of the aforementioned malady. Approaching my little rosebush, one might still have run the risk of being pricked.

Had I been negotiating with a layman, I would have had a few qualms about exposing him to repenting his amorous pursuit. But since I was dealing with a priest, the thought of fleecing him, without feeling the least bit uneasy about any consequences, was the only thing on my mind. Set a thief to catch a thief. The priestly profession consists of hoodwinkers operating under the hypocritical veil of Christian and social virtues. And since those charlatans preach for an *écu* things that they would not themselves do for a thousand times that sum, in a word, since those double-dealers have no other objective in this world than to grow fat, laughing all the while behind our backs, I thought I would commit an act more meritorious than reprehensible if I gave him something to remember me by. Thus, all things considered, I consented to see him, having decided that I would take him for everything he possessed, including his last collar, as soon as I could manage it.

Picture, if you will, a satyr as hairy as a Lycaon,[76] whose thin pale face announced a lustful disposition. Promiscuity and lasciviousness shone through the hypocrisy of his gaze. But let us leave his portrait unfinished, for fear that my description be the cause of a case of mistaken identity and that the perspicacious reader mistake Peter for Paul. I should never have expected that a man of the cloth could be quite as generous as was this particular priest. The first time we met, he offered me a gorgeous repeating watch by Julien Leroy,[77] beautifully engraved and set with diamonds. I have to admit to his credit that never did a churchman give better lie to the old proverb, 'as mean as a priest'. He was, on the contrary, so wildly extravagant that in less than two weeks he was forced to sell a living worth 2000 *écus*. He would have sold the entire clergy for me had I not passed on to him my little indisposition. As soon as he realized what had taken place, his love was transformed into rage, and, in a fit of anger, he almost raised his hands to strike me.

It was at that point that I relied on all the brazen impudence that women of my sort are capable of. I told him, with a firmness that shook him to the core, that I found it a bit rich on his part to insult me; that he deserved to be tossed out of a window; that my one and only mistake was to have been taken in by him in the first place; that I now perceived that received opinion concerning the clergy was not far off the mark, that most were incorrigible libertines and lechers, and that without a doubt, he picked up his little cupid's itch in some moll-house[78] or other. I added with considerable flourish that were it not for the vestige of pity in my breast, I would report him to the ecclesiastical court and that my word would carry enough weight to see him locked up; and lastly, that his punishment and penance would be in proportion to his immoral conduct. My vehement and terse disposition had the desired effect. The poor apostle was so shocked and humiliated that he decamped without a word and has never been heard from since.

Let this be a lesson to men of the cloth. May they learn that disgrace, opprobrium, and contempt are the usual reward for their scandalous conduct; may they learn to respect themselves if they would earn respect. Everyone knows that morals have little to do with one's garb, and that a lascivious appetite is not less clothed in the robes of a monk than in the suit of a layman. Still, certain iniquities are pardonable in a man of the world that are unforgivable in a man of the cloth. A priest is, after all, subject to certain rules of conduct from which the layman is excused. In a word, he must keep up appearances. Let him conceal his debauchery behind a facade of virtue and piety. His principal cunning lies in his ability to appear a true Christian in the eyes of the world and to thwart the designs of nature. For it is to nature alone, and not to his handiwork, that miracles belong. The churchman's responsibility is to be above suspicion. Good honest behaviour ought to shine out of all his actions. If, however, he takes others to be his fools, since he is paid to do so, I say, let him enjoy the benefit of his hypocrisy in peace.

The memento of my favours that I had left with Monsieur l'abbé convinced me more than ever that I must attend to my health. I scrupulously followed the doctor's orders and was soon enough back in the game. It is true that I did not have long to wait.

A Lord, or better still a 'Lourd', paid his homage to me in sterling, and then presented me with his miasmic vapours.[79] He was a stocky man who perfectly resembled a big toe. He walked like a duck and wore his sword crosswise like a Spaniard; his sword knot dangled down to his ankles. The qualities of his mind corresponded to those of his body; indeed, the two seemed made for one another, and one would have been hard pressed to choose one over the other. It may seem surprising that I have never had anyone under my thumb but that he was an irredeemable jackass. Need I point out that people of merit are not always rich, and that even when they are, they do not always seek out the company of the lady of pleasure? Only fools who have more money than sense beat a path to our door. And, in any event, since we are governed by self-interest alone, an old grunter, or even a monkey, so long as he has a purse full of money, is always sure to be better received than even the most agreeable young gent. Such is the power of money. Those who've got it outshine those who don't. Milord's guineas[80] transformed him. He became in my eyes a Lothario[81] who required that I observe a bizarre lifestyle in his company. We ate only grilled beef, mutton chops, and roast veal swimming in buttery gravy with bits of cabbage such as we feed to pigs in France. Sometimes (and this was his favourite dish) we had a slice of pork with apple marmalade. His palate was none too refined either. Burgundy, the best French wine, gave him heartburn. What he preferred was gut-rot that goes down rough, the kind of bad wine picklocks get drunk on. Then there was punch[§] and his pipes, for a true Englishman will not have properly dined without them. After dinner, when milord was gorged with drink, when he had smoked until he could smoke no more and belched like a hog, he fell asleep with his feet on the table. Were it not for the profits to be had, I could never have grown accustomed to such drunkenness and filth. Milord was generous and I fleeced him to my heart's content. I had only to denounce my compatriots, drink to the health of good King George and curse the Pope and the Pretender.[82] As long as I went along with these little eccentricities, I was free to empty his pockets.

One day, I was rewarded with more than three hundred *louis d'or* worth of goods for the price of a couple of toasts. I told him that I wanted to have a new dressing gown done up, and that, owing to his exquisite taste, he simply had to accompany me to a little shop in the rue Saint-Honoré.[83]

— Bless my heart, he cried. *Very well, yes, yes, very well.*[84] Your idea is very good, indeed. Advice in this matter will prove invaluable. By God, at first glance, I will tell you what suits best.

The reader will guess what modesty made me buy: two thirty-yard bolts of cloth, silver for the *pet-en-l'air*,[85] and gold for the dress front.

But this gift was nothing when compared to the prodigious quantity of cash I was able to extract from him. I had only to mention the glittering sums other gentlemen spent on their mistresses. Jealous emulation would make him try to spend even more. He could not bear the thought that any mortal being could be

[§] Drink made out of lemons, brandy, sugar and water.

more lavish in his spending than a subject of his Britannic Majesty. In four months, his foolish pride was worth 5000*l* in jewels and hard cash.

Is it possible that there are men so half-witted for the honour of their country that they will come to blows arguing about who spends the most on his mistress? As if the glory of a nation depended on the extravagance of a few dullards. Milord, whose figure was far from what one might call attractive, persisted in his high opinion of his physical strength. He claimed that no one in France could perform callisthenics with as much grace, strength, and agility as he could. He claimed to be an undisputed champion at leaping, wrestling, fencing, dancing, and riding... Yet, in reality, his execution of these various feats did not show his physical prowess in the most favourable light. Oftentimes, he would engage in mock sword-fights with Monsieur Gr — M — who, with the greatest aplomb, would deliver a blow with enough force to fell an ox, and which milord claimed not even to have felt! In order to avoid these pointless disputes, they agreed to mark the tips of their foil. Monsieur Gr — M — mixed some chimney soot and oil in which they both dipped the tips of their weapons. This done, they were soon at it, thrusting away until milord was hit in the middle of the chest. This time he could not argue that he had not felt the blow. The greasy smudge on his *jabot* was proof positive. Still, indignant to have received such a spectacular *mea culpa*, he charged all the harder, his mouth wide open, until Monsieur Gr — M —, getting carried away himself, shoved his blade down his adversary's throat. What was so unpleasant for milord was coughing up blood as black as Medusa's.[86] He lost two of his best teeth. In spite of this, nothing could curb or correct his intrepid courage, especially when he thought he might win the admiration of onlookers. This he soon proved in a scene no less risible and burlesque than the one I have just described.

We went with another couple for a drive in the *bois de Boulogne* in an open-top carriage. Milord felt the noble desire to show off his driving skill. He put the coachman in the back seat and humbly took the reins himself. As long as the road was wide without ruts, we trotted along at a fine clip. But having turned down a narrow lane, the noble driver needed all the dexterity he could muster to avoid a coach barrelling towards us. The swiftness with which the oncoming coach was approaching meant that milord scarcely had time to react. He gave the command in English to the horses. Now these were solid *Limousins*[87] with little experience of the world, and even less of foreign tongues. They therefore did the opposite of what they were commanded to do and crashed into the oncoming carriage, getting caught in the front wheels. The other driver, judging that milord was a rank beginner, gave him a crack of his whip with such force that he knocked the Englishman off his perch. Our Phaethon,[88] livid to have been knocked down, and doubly so to have been whipped, tore off his coat and challenged the Frenchman to fight it out. Strong and sinewy, the Frenchman gladly accepted the challenge. During this time, milord, bolder than Mars himself, struck his fighting pose, one foot behind the other and his fists doubled. The Frenchman, who was baffled by the Englishman's pose, tried to deliver a punch to the head, but the blow was deflected and answered in a flash with a strike to the face, then a second, then a third, each one more devastating than the last. Unaccustomed to this style of fighting, the Frenchman loses his balance and falls backward. Reassured that his nose is not broken and smoothing his mustachios, he rises ready to avenge his humiliation. The heroic Briton, solid as a rock, was preparing to knead his opponent's jaw and to give him a black eye or two when, unexpectedly, Monsieur La Violette (for that was the Frenchman's name) gratified him with a kick in the stomach, knocking the Englishman flat as a frog in the sand. Milord, purple with rage, cried foul and asked for his sword with which he intended to be done with the traitor. For our part, we could not see the merit of his grievance, especially as the kick appeared to us as good as a kick can be. When he finally calmed down, he explained that the rules governing the noble sport of pugilism strictly prohibited use of the feet.[89] We managed to appease his anger by insisting that such rules were completely unknown in France and that it had never occurred to anyone that it might be thought ungentlemanly to use all four limbs in cases like the present one. Satisfied by our arguments, he cheerily climbed back into his seat, overjoyed to have scored such a brilliant victory. It is true that he filled with admiration all who had witnessed this scene. The talent for pugilism is innate among the English. We French cannot hope to compete for the honour of being the greatest men on earth in the distinguished art of throwing a deft punch without being accused of foul play.

Soon after this martial adventure, domestic cares called milord back to England. He was naturally convinced that I would mind losing him and so, in order to console me and flatter my vanity, he maintained that the only things he would regret leaving in Paris were me and bull-baiting.[90]

By the time milord left Paris, I had accumulated enough capital to keep a proper house and while away the days in delicious luxury and repose. I nonetheless was aware that one's appetite for riches grows in proportion to the riches one has already acquired. Miserliness and hoarding invariably go along with wealth. The desire to reap rewards, in other words, the hope of one day savouring those rewards without constraint, pushes back the moment when one might feel free to spend. Our wants increase with our income; we find ourselves in need, though surrounded with opulence. I already had an annual income of 12,000*l*. I did not want to contemplate retiring until I had at least 20,000*l*. True enough, for a girl as highly sought after as I was, this was not an unreasonable ambition. The recent favours that fortune had bestowed upon me proved to my mind that I could expect more. My Englishman had not yet reached Dover before one of the forty immortals of the *Hôtel des Fermes*[§][91] took his place. I received

[§] The author uses this ironic expression because there are forty farmers general (regional tax collectors) and forty members of the French Academy.

him with all the courtesy owed to his strong box. Without being overcome by the honour he paid me, I explained that I had been for a time exclusively devoted to foreign affairs, and that as soon as a worthy foreigner happened along, our lease would be null and void. He accepted the terms and the agreement was signed.

He was a tall man, well enough made with a face not unpleasant. He was, nevertheless, like the majority of tax collectors, an insufferable prig. The earth itself was unworthy of his feet. He had a sovereign disregard for everyone but himself. He believed himself a universal genius. He spoke on all subjects as if he were an expert, and contradicted anyone who might hold a different view. And God help anyone who might contradict him! He wanted to be listened to but cared not to listen to anyone else. In a word, the bully came down like a ton of bricks on the most mild-mannered people and then expected to be applauded for his intimidating ways.

One good thing he accomplished in setting up shop was to reform the deplorable taste milord had introduced in my kitchen and to re-establish in its place rich and succulent meals worthy of a baron of high finance. Morning and night the table was laid for eight, six of whom were poets, painters or musicians and who, in the interest of their hungry stomachs, dispensed their flowery blandishments at the feet of my Croesus.[92] My house became a tribunal where art and talent were discussed and judged no less sovereignly than in Madame de T's literary canteen,[93] where, as everyone knows, all the best authors are chewed up and spat out. As it happened, in my salon, indulgence was poured on second-rate scribblers. Oftentimes, preference was given to their work. Still, it is a bit much to listen to Grub Street tear to shreds the inimitable letters of the author of the *Temple de Gnide*[§][94] and then take pot shots at poor abbé Pélegrin[95] for having rightly pointed out that the *Lettres juives* are little more than a monstrous compilation of incongruous thoughts shamelessly lifted from Bayle,[96] Le Clerc's *Bibliothèque universelle*,[97] the *Espion turc*,[98] and so on — a compilation, moreover, hopelessly disfigured, and badly expressed in Provençal patois.[99] This latter priest, who had little against him, save poverty and filth, was possessed of a great soul in a dirty body. The poor man had to put up with sarcasm and insults for his whole life; he, nevertheless, had excellent judgement. Abbé Pélegrin taught me the fundamentals of good taste, and it is entirely because of his influence that I have been spared the dreadful infection known as fashionable wit. For instance, it is he who opened my eyes to the vanity and pettiness of literary hacks, and who brought me to understand that authentic discernment is a pure and sacred flame, a gift from heaven that cannot be acquired. Finally, abbé Pélegrin taught me that one must be wary not to confuse the true genius with the multitude of lackeys known for their facetious wit, a quality that people of taste view as a blemish on

[§] *Lettres persanes* by M. de Montesquieu.

the profession of letters, which, although a noble profession, is nowadays brought into disrepute by the swarms of insects settling on it.

— You will never guess, he told me one day, why Paris is so overrun with this cursed mob. It is because it is a profession that requires neither talent nor wit. To see for yourself, teach your coachman a few fashionable phrases. Send him down to the *Procope*[100] for a month or two. I guarantee that he will come back as fatuous and self-satisfied as all the others. Alas! he added with a deep sigh, my parents are to blame for all the ridicule and hardships I have had to suffer. The brutes forced me as a tender youth to take religious orders with the Servite Friars.[101] The repugnance I felt for religious life increased with age. I suffered for years in a monk's cowl. I would have died of despair had I not found the means to have myself secularized.[102] Without friends, with no money, and lacking the means to support myself, freedom soon became an intolerable burden. I almost reached the point where I regretted my former fetters. Not knowing what to do, I ended up here. In the beginning, I subsisted by saying mass and by running off sermons which I sold to the mendicant orders.[103] Needy and with little to do, I could not afford to be particular about the company I kept. I frequented a tobacco parlour near the *Foire Saint-Germain*[104] where there gathered acrobats, puppeteers, a few actors from the *Opéra Comique*, and, among others, the sieur Colin, famed playhouse snuffer.[105] These new friends gave me complimentary tickets to their performances. Theatre fever took hold of me, and I soon had the itch to write for the stage. I wrote a few bad scenes and was paid too much for them. I would have liked to conciliate my sacred duties with those of a playwright, but the Archbishop of Paris decided to deprive me of these easy pickings by relieving me of my priestly charge. I lost 15 sous a day, almost all of the income I earned by saying mass. In order to make up for the loss, I set up shop as a poet and busied myself writing comedies, operas and tragedies which I had performed under my brother's name, or which I sold to anyone wishing to pass himself off as an author. Yes, indeed, all manner of writings: flowery verse, marriage songs, hymns and sermons. I sold them all wholesale or retail. I can assure you that more than one member of that illustrious Bedlam housed in the old Louvre[§] did not hesitate to humble himself at my boutique in search of an appropriate reception speech. One would think that with such a thriving business, I should be rich. Judge for yourself. For more than fifty years, I have composed millions of lines, and I have not a pair of drawers to my name.

[§] *L'Académie française* (The French Academy).

The air of candour and naiveté with which Pélegrin recounted his life convinced me that of all professions that of the scribbler, the work-for-hire writer, is the most thankless and the most haphazard. His true merit nevertheless convinced me that there are happy men in the profession of letters, as in any other profession, and that there are plenty of writers who owe their good name to their lucky star, rather than to their talent. How many jumped-up celebrities strut about Paris? One might never have heard their name but for the protection of some court potentate, or high-flying strumpet. How many have I known who, by virtue of the powers that be, occupy the first rank among Apollo's disciples,[106] yet who are simply incapable of pulling out of their brains a fraction of the good things abbé Pélegrin has written? All flattering comparisons aside, the poor devil resembled a carnival merry-andrew.[107] People laugh at him but, in truth, he is infinitely more acute than his tormentors. Let us conclude that merit goes to waste when it is not seconded by Fortune, for it is Fortune that makes men great. Nature provides only the outline.

Back to my blue-ribbon financier. He was designated by the firm to do the rounds and inspect the regional agents under his authority to ensure that they were performing their duties properly: that is to say, oppressing and robbing the public, and looking for new ways to ride rough shod over the same. We therefore broke our contract by mutual consent, and went our separate ways.

I should have responded a while ago to a question that readers will doubtless have asked themselves many times over. How is it that Margot, whose libidinous nature resembles that of the Empress Messalina,[108] could consent to see men for money, men who were for the most part no great shakes in bed?

Nothing could be more pertinent than this question, and it is reasonable, gentlemen, that I try to offer an explanation. Know then that, following the examples of the Duchesses of the old court, and several of my associates in the trade, I always had in my employ, but please, this must remain a secret, I have always had in my household a young vigorous footman. This arrangement suits me so well that I have every intention of adhering to it as long as my heart beats in my breast. Besides being of no account, these fellows are always on call. Unlike certain men of distinction, they rarely fail to give satisfaction. When they do have difficulty performing in bed, it would be unjust and cruel to make them suffer for it. If they get uppity, it is easy to take care of that. A few whacks with a stick, you pay them their wages and, farewell, without a fuss. It is true that it almost never comes to that because I always take the precaution of recruiting fresh young swains, exactly the same in body and mind as the peasants portrayed by Marivaux, naïve and light-hearted.[109] I educate them myself and make them do as I please. I do not tolerate them to associate with their fellows for fear that the scoundrels corrupt their innocence and lead them astray. I keep their nose to the grindstone. In any event, they want for nothing. They are well looked after and fed like caged chickens or, to speak less metaphorically, like a nun's confessor who has not a care in the world, save producing in his charges devotedly good chyle[110] and performing the requisite duties that go along with that. There, gentlemen, now you know how I hold my appetite for lasciviousness in check. This reasonable system means that my little pleasures are never bitter. I enjoy them in peace, with no fanfare, without having to worry about an imperious lover's bad moods or his lack of constancy, a lover who, treating me like a slave, would make me pay for his caresses out of my own savings and leave me destitute. I am not one of those foolish love-struck girls. It goes without saying that everyone is free to cultivate noble sentiments and platonic affection. I don't feed on fine feelings. Refined emotion and convoluted sentiments don't suit me. My constitution requires stronger food. Truly, Mr Plato was an eccentric with his theories about love.[111] Where would humankind be today if people had gone along with the bird-brained schemes of that bungler? Nature did not endow him with understanding any better than Origen;[112] he may even have lacked something like Eloise's lover.[113] One thing is for sure, he did not learn his metaphysics from his teacher Socrates, who had all the bits you need and without which you cannot become Pope.[114] Plato was put on the right track, but at some point he was otherwise distracted. Back to our story.

News of my 'widowhood' had hardly been made public before I was beleaguered by a multitude of fools of every conceivable size, shape and description. An ambassador extraordinary delivered me from this constant torment. I could scarce hide from myself the joy I felt having made a conquest of this magnitude. What a triumph! My vanity was rightly flattered. Imagine how satisfied I was to see at my feet a man whose skill managed the most subtle minds with shrewdness, and with a perfect knowledge of the interests of the crowned heads of Europe, who, with the stroke of a pen, could influence international affairs and, in so doing, contribute greatly to the well-being of his country. Such was the portrait I imagined of His Excellency before I saw him. I had no doubt that these rare and sublime talents would be seconded by a thousand other qualities, for I naturally assumed that a man who had been promoted to such an exalted post must have been endowed with superior gifts.

What convinced me that this must be the case was the way he conducted himself with respect to me. Our agreement was reached through lengthy negotiations. Secret agents approached me on his behalf. I sent my own *envoyés*. They deliberated. Proposals were listened to, examined, debated. Each camp was naturally looking to advance its own interests; negotiations dragged on. Difficulties were imagined where none existed. Having reached an agreement on one point, there were disagreements on another. At length, after several conferences dismissed and then reconvened, our plenipotentiaries signed all the articles and a double treaty was exchanged to our mutual satisfaction.

Having reason to suppose that the reader is anxious to meet His Excellency, I shall, without further ado, give a full description. Monsieur l'Ambassadeur had one of those faces you could call unassuming and thus difficult to describe. He was slightly taller than the average, neither well nor ill made. He had the legs of a man of quality: that is to say, thin and bony. He affected a noble air at variance with his common-looking face. He held his head high, puffed out his cheeks and continually eyed the ribbon in his lapel. His demeanour was silent and introspective. One could easily have surmised that he was pondering deep thoughts and calculating vast schemes. He almost never spoke, in order to make one think he spent a great deal of time thinking and, moreover, that his disposition required circumspection and calculated speech. If questioned, he responded with a vague shaking of the head accompanied by a mysterious wink and an imperceptible little smile. Who would believe that with such a bizarre exterior and such an ambivalent demeanour, I was, for a whole month, besotted with the idea that he was the greatest man in the world? That is, until such time as his secretary drew me the following charitable portrait. I have already indicated that our servants are our most uncompromising censors. If the ignorant ones are aware of our little faults, imagine trying to escape the biting sarcasm of those with a bit of penetration. The secretary in question was too acute to be easily taken in by his master's scowl and studied mien. I found his comments judicious and, to court the reader, I will relay them. The secretary speaks thus:

— Remember, says he to me, in order not to be taken in by the great of this world, one must understand that their greatness is an effect of our insignificance. Blind and pusillanimous respect raises them in our esteem. Dare look them in the eye, and take away their tawdry trappings: their prestige immediately vanishes. Thus you see them for their intrinsic worth. You will also see that what you took for grandeur and dignity was at best pride and fatuity. A maxim to remember: personal merit is no more proportional to the importance of one's station than is the goodness of a horse is to the richness of its harness. Bridle a nag, give it all the trappings, and let it pull the most elegant carriage. None of these gewgaws will transform the nag. It will still be a nag. The proof of the pudding is in the eating. An intellect as narrow as His Excellency's imagines that to be a Minister of State, it is enough to project an air of discretion, a grave and controlled exterior, an imperious, haughty bearing. As far as I am concerned, such a man is a bumptious twit. He can puff himself up as much as he pleases, strut and carry his head high; it is easy enough to see in such forced airs his attempt to hide incompetence. Such a man is out of his depth. As soon as he is out of the public eye, he does not hesitate to shift his responsibilities to us. And what, pray tell, do you think he does while we sweat trying to decipher and answer dispatches? He dawdles with the servants, his pet monkey, and his dogs. He makes cut-outs and sings a ditty, plays the flute, lolls in an armchair, stretches, and yawns, and falls asleep.

> Please do not imagine that all ministers are modelled on this one. There are some whose merit is infinitely above praise. I know several who have not only the talents one would expect in a Minister of State, but also the ability to inspire warmth and affection and general esteem, and who, so different from their bogus colleagues, know how to work in private and how to relax in company. These are accomplished politicians whose self-confidence and frankness inspire trust and to whom no one would hesitate to open his heart or to speak his mind.

His Excellency's secretary told me many more interesting things that I could insert here, but since everything becomes tedious if dwelt on at too great length, I prefer to leave the reader wanting to hear more.

Soon thereafter, the admiration and respect that I once had for His Excellency turned into contempt. In spite of his splendour and largesse, I would have been capable of any misdemeanour in order to end our affair. As it turns out, my declining health provided the perfect pretext. I fell into an extreme lethargy and melancholy that perplexed the most celebrated doctors. None could diagnose the disease from which I suffered, and each had his own theory, backed up with such decisive syllogisms that I thought myself suffering from several maladies at the same time. I swallowed medicine by the bucketful. My body was now an apothecary's boutique. I had lost so much weight that I was but a shadow of my former self. I struggled in vain to replace my plumpness and the natural bloom of my complexion with paint and padding. Rouge, creams, powder and patches were not enough to bring back Margot's pretty face. After two hours spent in front of my looking-glass, and only with the utmost effort, was I able to perceive the vaguest outline of my former beauty. I began to resemble a prop in the theatre: beautiful from a distance, but perfectly hideous up close. The layers of make-up I applied to my face gave me panache, but on close inspection I was a mess of coarse colours, offensive to the eyes. Alackaday! I was doubly afflicted when I recalled the days when Margot was innocent of a woman's little tricks and refinements, when, in a word, I was independently rich and only borrowed my charms from myself.

I was so consumed by my ills that I was convinced I was dying on my feet when an experimental doctor, or quack, to whom was given the nickname 'Aim-for-the-eye', because he claimed that he could diagnose any ill by looking in the patient's eye, was brought to my attention. Although I have never had any faith in miracle workers, my present weakness inclined me greatly toward credulity. And since there is nothing one believes more readily than that which one desires ardently, I asked Dr Aim-for-the-eye to pass by my house. At first glance, his physiognomy reassured me greatly. He had a gracious air of openness rather than the disquieting expression of the majority of doctors and quacks. He started by asking for an honest account of my past life before I fell ill and the treatment I had been following since. After which, having looked into my eyes fixedly for two or three minutes without moving or breathing a word, he broke the silence with these words.

— Mademoiselle, you are fortunate that the doctors did not kill you. Your illness, which they were never able to diagnose, has nothing to do with the body. It is, rather, an affliction of the mind caused by too much pleasure. Pleasure is to the soul what rich food is to the stomach. The most exquisite dishes soon become insipid if we eat them too often; then they are disgusting, since we can no longer digest them. An excess of pleasure has stupefied your heart and enervated your feelings. In spite of all the delights of your present situation, everything is intolerable. Tiresome worries follow you everywhere. Even on the most joyous occasions, pleasure is a torment. Such is your state. If you want my advice, keep away from noisy company. Eat only healthy solid food. Go to bed early, and rise early as well. Take plenty of exercise and do not frequent those whose temperament is not aligned with yours. But mostly, stop taking these blasted medicines. In six weeks, I guarantee you will be as beautiful and fresh as ever.

Dr Aim-for-the-eye's words had such a marvellous effect on my nerves that if I believed in conjuration, I would have thought that he had just touched me with a magic wand. It seemed as if I were waking from a deep sleep during which I dreamt that I had been ill. Persuaded that I owed my life to Dr Aim-for-the-eye, I embraced him before dismissing him with a gift of 12 *louis d'or*.

I was resolved to observe rigorously doctor's orders and so, my first duty was to signify my intention to resign from the Opera. It is normal procedure to give six months' notice, but Monsieur Thuret waived this formality. I was no sooner free than, for the first time since leaving home, I began to wonder about my parents' whereabouts. It is true that I had carried on as if they never existed, as if I had fallen from the sky. The sudden change in my fortunes brought them to mind. I felt guilty that I had behaved with ingratitude toward them, and I set about to make up for lost time, that is, if they were still alive. For a long time my search was fruitless. An old merchant informed me that Monsieur Tranche-montagne ended his days manning the oars in a galley out of Marseille, and that my mother was for the time being incarcerated at the *Salpêtrière*,[115] having beforehand received a public thrashing from the hand of Monsieur de Paris.

I found their lot touching. Far from blaming them for having ended up so pitifully, I could not help justifying them in my heart, recalling Maître Pathelin's[116] comment that it is difficult to be respectable when one is poor. How many people who pass for goodness incarnate because they have everything their heart desires would have done worse under similar circumstances? There is nothing in this world but good and ill fortune. The unlucky get caught; if everyone who deserved punishment were strung up, the population would be thinned out soon enough.

Convinced that this is the case, I used all my personal influence to have my mother released, in the expectation that thereupon she would be just as respectable as anyone else. Thank God, I was right! Today she is one of the most thoughtful people I know. She is my housekeeper, and I have to say to her credit that the house has never been run better. If I have contributed to her well-being, I can say that she has contributed to mine in eager and sincere anticipation of my every desire.

We divide our time between town and country, and enjoy with a few intimate friends the best that life has to offer. As for my health, it is now perfectly sound, with the exception of the odd bout of insomnia. Since Dr Aim-for-the-eye has banned all medicine, I began reading before bed a few pages of the narcotic works of the marquis d'Argens,[117] the chevalier de Mouhy,[118] and several other excellent writers, with the result that I now sleep like a baby. I recommend this method to all those who have trouble sleeping. Upon my word, they will feel much better.

Finally, I feel I must respond to the accusation that I have been too free in my descriptions. This is the reason why: I believe that the best way to decry the whore is to portray her in the worst possible light, and to have her slowly pass through the most abominable trials. Whatever the reader's sentiment, I take pride in the fact that the obscenities in these memoirs will prove instructive to young people making their way in the world. They can now give some thought to the sly little games played by whores, and consider the great danger that comes in frequenting their company. If this book fulfils that purpose, so much the better. If not, I wash my hands of it.

Notes

1. **General de la Pousse**: code name for Nicolas René Berryer (1703–1762), magistrate and politician famous for his tenure as *lieutenant de la police* (1747–1757). Joseph d'Hémery (1722–1806), inspector of books and printing, worked directly under Berryer. 'Pousse' here signifies 'bumbailiff'.
2. **Rue Saint-Paul**: street in the old working-class east end of Paris. Perpendicular to the rue Saint-Antoine, it leads to the Seine and owes its name to St Paul's parish church.
3. **Rue Saint-Antoine**: broad east-west axis starting at the Bastille and leading to the rue des Barres near the *Hôtel de Ville*. Its proximity to the Bastille made the rue Saint-Antoine the site of many popular uprisings.
4. **Tester**: canopy over a bed, pulpit or altar.
5. **Cythera**: Aphrodite, Greek goddess of love. According to myth, it was in the waters off Cythera (Crete) that Aphrodite rose out of the aphrós (αφρός) — foam — after Uranus's genitals had been cast into the sea.
6. **La Rapée**: village just outside the walls of old Paris on the right bank of the Seine (near today's Bercy in the 12th arrondissement). Away from prying eyes, Parisians could indulge in sundry pleasures, including the ones recorded here.
7. **Priapus** (Πρίαπος): minor god of fertility, protector of livestock, fruit plants, gardens and male genitalia.
8. **Grève**: square in the 4th arrondissement of Paris (now *Place de l'Hôtel de Ville*). The French word *grève* refers to the gravelled area on the shores of a body of water. The location occupied by the square today was once a sandy beach and site of the city's riverine harbour (the *quai de Grève*, built in 1673). The *Place de la Grève* was used as a public meeting-place and also as a site where the unemployed gathered: hence the French word *grève* meaning strike. The *Place de la Grève* is also remembered as the traditional site of the city's public executions.
9. **Pont Royal**: third oldest bridge in Paris (after the *Pont Neuf* and the *Pont Marie*), constructed by command of Louis XIV between 1685 and 1689. The *Pont Royal* links the right bank by the *Pavillon de Flore* (Louvre) with the left bank at the rue du Bac.
10. **Tuileries**: royal palace on the right bank of the Seine begun by Catherine de Medici in 1564 and destroyed during the Commune in 1871. The Tuileries presented an imposing west façade, gradually extended until it closed off the Louvre courtyard. The reference here is to the Tuileries Gardens designed by Le Nôtre in 1664. In 1667, at the request of Charles Perrault, the author of *Sleeping Beauty* and other fairy tales, the Tuileries were opened to the public. Excluded were beggars, lackeys, soldiers, and, presumably, street prostitutes.
11. **Terrace des Capucins**: designed by Le Nôtre on the westernmost side of the Tuileries Gardens, named for the garden of the Capucin friars, whose convent was located nearby.
12. **Well-dressed lady**: contemporary reports specify that only well-dressed persons were allowed to enter the Tuileries. See note 10 above.
13. **Saint-Cloud**: suburb to the west of Paris famous for its sixteenth-century *château*, destroyed during the Franco-Prussian war (1870). Boasting an immense park, Saint-Cloud was a favourite summertime destination for Parisians in search of fresh air. In 1658 the château belonged to the Orléans branch of the French royal family. It was bought in 1785 by Louis XVI for Marie-Antoinette, who was convinced that the air of Saint-Cloud would be good for her children.
14. **Madame Lacroix's**: located on the *Terrace des Feuillants* (see note 15). During the eighteenth century this café was known under a number of names: *le café des Tuileries, le café Payen, le café Hottot*, etc.
15. **Porte des Feuillants**: one of the six gates giving access to the old Tuileries Gardens, situated

on the north side of the gardens and opening onto the rue Le Manège (today rue de Rivioli).

16. **Rue Montmartre**: ancient north-south axis extending from Montmartre to the *Halles*.
17. **Escoffion**: head-dress popular in France in the mid-sixteenth century, shaped like an oval hood worn at the back of the head, and showing off the forehead.
18. **Our two heroines were at each other's throats**: for a similar women's battle see Fielding's *Tom Jones*, Book IV Ch. 8: 'A battle sung by the muse in the Homerican style, and which none but the classical reader can taste'.
19. **Madame Florence**: Césarine Florence (dates unknown), celebrated madam known to have run several bawdy houses in the 1740s.
20. **Maid**: virgin.
21. **Ointments**: myrtle water (or *eau de pucelle*), believed to restore the appearance of virginity.
22. **Furbelows**: a gathered strip or pleated border of a skirt or petticoat.
23. **My other maidenhead**: euphemism for anal penetration.
24. **Supererogation**: the act of performing more than is required by duty, obligation, or need. The judge here speaks the language of jurisprudence.
25. **Synod**: a council of a church, convened to decide an issue of doctrine or administration.
26. **Bidet**: basin used since the seventeenth century to wash the genitalia. In Old French, *bider* meant to trot. One sits astride a bidet the same way one rides a pony.
27. See the later *Candide*, Ch. 24: (the prostitute Paquette speaks) 'Ah! sir, if you could only imagine what it is to be obliged to fondle an old merchant, a lawyer, a monk, a gondolier, and an abbé with the same show of affection; to be exposed to abuse and insults; to have to borrow a skirt just so that some disagreeable old geezer can lift it up; to be robbed by one man of what you've earned from another; to be fleeced by the officers of justice, and to have no prospect in view but frightful old age, the workhouse and pauper's grave, you would conclude that I am one of the most unhappy creatures in the world' (my translation).
28. **Martin**: Robert Martin (1706–1765), the King's 'varnisher' (1733). *Vernis Martin* is a generic name given to a brilliant translucent lacquer used in the decoration of furniture, carriages, sedan chairs and small articles such as snuff-boxes and fans.
29. **Worshipping at the altar of Silenus**: drinking. In Greek mythology, Silenus (Σειληνός) was the elderly companion of the wine god Dionysus.
30. **Refrigerative**: medicine intended to lower a fever. Remedy for syphilis which involved 'cooling' the blood with diuretics.
31. **Rue d'Argentueil**: street in the 1st arrondissement of Paris north of the *Palais-Royal*, built on the old road to Argenteuil, now a north-western suburb of Paris.
32. **Bicêtre**: originally planned as a veteran's hospital south of Paris (1634). With the help of Vincent de Paul, it opened as an orphanage in 1642. By the early eighteenth century *Bicêtre* was a lunatic asylum as well as a hospital and a prison for undesirables (e.g. beggars, vagabonds, prostitutes and homosexuals). Until 1780, all suspected cases of venereal infection were sent to *Bicêtre* for treatment. See notes 34, 35 below.
33. ***Hic et nunc***: here and now, immediately.
34. **Efficacious grease**: (pun on 'efficacious Grace'). This was in fact mercury ointment, the traditional treatment for the symptoms of syphilis.
35. **St Cosimo's mercury baths**: supposed cure for syphilis. St Cosimo is patron of surgeons. In popular lore, he was patron saint of venereal infection. See note 34.
36. **Pasiphaë** (Πασιφαής 'wide-shining'): in Greek mythology, daughter of Helios, the Sun. Her lust for a white bull, sent by Poseidon, consecrated her reputation for bestiality and the supposed shocking excesses of female sensuality.
37. **Mademoiselle Joly**: evidently a kept woman of some notoriety. Not to be confused with Marie-Elisabeth Joly (1761–1798) of the *Comédie Française*.

38. **Chaste Susannah**: in the Old Testament book of Daniel, wife of Joakim, at whose house the elders of the Jews met. On their way to a meeting, two judges secretly observed Susanna taking her bath in the garden. They threatened to tell that she was meeting a young man in the garden if she did not make love with them. She refused. This story is considered as an example of the triumph of virtue.
39. **Grey musketeer**: the musketeers of the King's Household formed two regiments, one mounted on black horses and the other on grey.
40. **Rue du Chantre**: street near the old Louvre. Monbron himself was living in the rue du Chantre at the time of his arrest in November 1748.
41. **Fontainebleau**: royal country house sixty kilometres south east of Paris. The construction of Fontainebleau was undertaken by the great builder-king, Francis I (1494–1547), who, in the largest of his many construction projects, reconstructed, expanded, and transformed the royal château at Fontainebleau. From the sixteenth to the eighteenth century, every monarch, from Francis I to Louis XV, made important renovations to Fontainebleau.
42. **Striking the sleeping couple**: for a similar scene see Fielding's *Tom Jones*, Book IX Ch. 6: 'Containing, among other things, the ingenuity of Partridge, the madness of Jones, and the folly of Fitzpatrick'.
43. **Aretino**: Pietro Aretino (1492–1556), Italian author, playwright, poet, satirist, and blackmailer. In his celebrated *Ragionamenti* (Reasonings), the sex lives of wives, prostitutes and nuns are compared and contrasted. The dialogue concludes that all women (regardless of condition) must submit to having sexual relations and that, under these conditions, it is best to become a prostitute and at least be paid for one's efforts.
44. **Clinchtel (or Clinchetel)**: Karl Gustav Klingstedt (1657–1734), Swedish miniaturist and enamellist specializing in gallant scenes. Klingstedt lived in Paris from 1677 until his death. His style was referenced by many literary figures including Voltaire, La Harpe, Bernard and others.
45. **Prebendary's stipend**: the stipend given to the curate of a cathedral or collegiate church.
46. **Rue Champ-fleuri**: street (now demolished) leading from the rue Saint-Honoré to the garden of the old Louvre, reputedly frequented by prostitutes.
47. **Seraphic order of St Francis**: order of Friars Minor, or Franciscans.
48. **Ruins of a church**: the roof of *Saint-Thomas-du-Louvre* collapsed on 15 December 1739. Monbron's note would put the publication date of *Margot* at 1753.
49. **Procurer**: a person who obtains a woman as a prostitute for another person: pimp.
50. **Oven**: Dutch or common oven for use outside the home.
51. **Neuilly**: western suburb of Paris.
52. **Aspergillum**: liturgical implement used to sprinkle holy water.
53. **Tenon and mortise**: joint used for thousands of years by woodworkers to join pieces of wood. A mortise is a cavity cut into a timber to receive a tenon.
54. **Opera**: *Académie Royale de Musique, Salle du Palais-Royal*, built 1641; altered 1660, 1671, and 1674; destroyed by fire on 6 April 1763.
55. **Socratiser**: originally, to moralize in the manner of Socrates. The obscene meaning of the word is attested since the mid-eighteenth century. See *La Nouvelle Justine* in Sade, *Œuvres*, ed. by Michel Delon and Jean Deprun (Paris: Gallimard, Bibliothèque de la Pléiade, 1995), vol 2, p. 1332.
56. **Monsieur Thuret**: Louis Armand Eugène de Thuret (birth?–1762), director of the Opera (1733–1744).
57. **Malterre le Diable**: François-Louis Malter (1699–1788), dancer in the *ballets du Roi*, member of the *Académie royale de danse*, son of François-Antoine. François-Louis was called le Diable (the Devil) because he excelled in the portrayal of demons.
58. **Opéra Comique**: a more popular art form than formal opera, combining vaudeville and comedy, both the high and low, the *Théâtre de l'Opéra-Comique* was founded in 1714. In

Monbron's time it was installed in a wing of the *Hôtel des Menus-Plaisirs* on the rue Bergère in today's 9th arrondissement.

59. **Rue Sainte-Anne**: fashionable street, perpendicular to the rue Saint-Honoré and running parallel to the Palais-Royal, built in the early seventeenth century and named in honour of Anne of Austria, Queen of France.
60. **Mademoiselle Durocher**: Marie Durocher (dates unknown), famous courtesan. The Lord Weymouth named here is Thomas Thynne (1710–1751), second Viscount Weymouth.
61. **Timeo danaos et dons ferentes**: 'I fear the Greeks even when they bring gifts', Virgil, *Aeneid* II, 49. The gift in question is syphilis.
62. **Jephté** (Jephtha): opera by the French composer Michel Pignolet de Montéclair (1667–1737). The opera takes the form of a *tragédie en musique* (French lyric tragedy) in a prologue and five acts. The libretto, by the abbé Simon-Joseph Pellegrin, is based on the Biblical story of Jephtha (Judges 12). See note 95 below.
63. **Monsieur de La Frenaie** (dates unknown): celebrated jeweller who also appears in Diderot's *Bijoux indiscrets* under the name of Frénicol. The name lends itself to a play on words: frénésie = frenzy (for jewels).
64. **Croix à la devote**: pectoral cross worn as a piece of jewellery. See 'croix' in Diderot's *Encyclopédie.*
65. **Place Vendôme**: imposing square north of the Tuileries gardens, laid out in 1702 as a monument to the glory of the armies of Louis XIV.
66. **Tournoi**: or *livre* (pound).
67. **Snuff-box à la Maubois**: Jeanne-Madeleine Maubois (1686–1777): artist in ivory and tortoiseshell, named *tourneuse du Roy.*
68. **Arquebuse water**: spirituous water, supposedly useful in cases of gun-shot wounds (*arquebuse*: sixteenth-century term for rifle).
69. **Mademoiselle Durocher**: Marie Durocher (dates unknown). The incident referred to here is obscure.
70. **Palais-Royal**: originally built for Richelieu and called the *Palais-Cardinal* (1633–1639), the *Palais-Royal* was a royal residence located in the 1st arrondissement of Paris, opposite the Louvre. Situated near the *Opéra*, its gardens were notorious in the eighteenth century as a gathering place for kept women.
71. **Quinze-Vingts**: hospice founded in 1260 by Saint Louis, located near the Louvre in rue Saint-Honoré at the corner of the rue Saint-Nicaise. The French name *Quinze-Vingts* means three hundred (15 × 20 = 300) and referred to the number of beds in the hospital. From the end of the Middle Ages onward, the *Quinze-Vingts* was a hospital for the blind.
72. **Bois de Boulogne**: woodland and pleasure ground to the west of Paris.
73. **Glacière**: warehouse located outside Paris (13th arrondissement) where formerly ice from the river *Bièvre* was stockpiled and stored for use during the summer.
74. **Roman d'Astrée**: pastoral novel by Honoré d'Urfé, published between 1607 and 1627, and an influential work of seventeenth-century French literature.
75. **Mademoiselle Pellicier** (1707–1749): French opera singer famous in the 1720s and 1730s. Her 1729 love affair with the Portuguese Jew, François Lopès Dulis (Ulysse), for which she received a fortune in diamonds, ended badly. Warned that his lover was unfaithful, Dulis wanted his diamonds back. The ensuing scandal resulted in a play by Abbé Desfontaines, *Le Triomphe de l'intérêt*, performed in 1730. See Desforges, *Mémoires, anecdotes pour servir à l'histoire de M. Duliz, fameux Juif portugais* (La Haye, 1739); *Et la suite de ses avantures, aprés la catastrophe de celle de Mademoiselle Pelissier, actrice de l'Opéra de Paris* (London: Harding, 1739).
76. **Lycaon** (Λυκάων): king of Arcadia who, in the most popular version of the myth, tested Zeus's omniscience by serving him the roasted flesh of a guest, in return for which Zeus transformed him into a wolf.

77. **Julien Leroy** (1686–1759): Parisian watchmaker.
78. **Moll-house**: brothel.
79. **Miasmic vapours**: reference to the supposed English inclination toward a saturnine or gloomy disposition. The play on words 'Lord-Lourd', 'lourd' meaning heavy, is well-known.
80. **Guinea**: gold coin minted in Great Britain between 1663 and 1814. Originally worth one pound sterling, equal to twenty shillings; from 1717 until 1816, its value was officially fixed at twenty-one shillings. Replaced by the sovereign in 1816, the guinea had an aristocratic flavour. Professional fees and payment for land, horses, art, bespoke tailoring, furniture and other luxury items were often quoted in guineas until a couple of years after decimalization in 1971.
81. **Lothario**: name which connotes an unscrupulous seducer of women after *La Novela del curioso impertinente* by Cervantes (1605). In English literature see Nicholas Rowe's play *The Fair Penitent* (1703).
82. **Drink to the health of good King George**: French novels in the period frequently refer to the English custom of toasting the King. The Pretender named here is Prince Charles Edward Stuart (1720–1788), second Jacobite pretender to the thrones of England, Scotland, and Ireland.
83. **Rue Saint-Honoré**: upmarket east-west axis in the 1st arrondissement of Paris, laid out in the Middle Ages.
84. **Very well, yes, yes, very well.** English in the original. See Mrs Western speaking French in Fielding's *Tom Jones*, Book XV, Ch. 6.
85. **Pet-en-l'air**: a cross between a jacket and a skirt (the word 'pet' means fart). The fart-in-the-air was an eighteenth-century women's garment, worn on the hips in ample skirt-like pleats.
86. **Medusa** (Μέδουσα: 'guardian, protectress'): in Greek mythology Medusa was a monster, a Gorgon, generally described as having the face of a hideous human female with living venomous snakes in place of hair. Gazing directly into her eyes would turn onlookers to stone.
87. **Limousins**: ancient breed of saddle horse from the Limousin region of France, now extinct.
88. **Phaethon** (Φαέθων: shining one): in Greek mythology, son of Clymene and the solar deity Helios. The French form of the name 'Phaethon' is 'Phaéton'. This form of the word is applied to a type of horse-drawn carriage, and hence to the carriage driver.
89. **Boxing**: see Fielding, *Tom Jones*, Book XIII, Ch. 5.
90. **Bull-baiting** (*Combat du taureau*): a bloody spectacle closer to bear-baiting than the modern art of bull-fighting. In eighteenth-century Paris the *combat du taureau* did not involve humans, but rather the bull being torn to bits by dogs or wild boars in an arena. The *Combat des Animaux* was a stadium located in the rue de Sèvres. See Pierre-Louis Manuel, *La Police de Paris dévoilée* (Paris: Garnery, 1794), vol. 2, pp. 296–97.
91. **Hôtel des Fermes**: located near the Louvre, formerly the central tax collection office established by Colbert in 1681.
92. **Croesus** (Κροῖσος, 595 BC–*c.* 547 BC): king of Lydia from 560 to 547 BC until his defeat by the Persians. In Greek and Persian cultures the name of Croesus became a synonym for a very wealthy man.
93. **Madame de T's literary canteen**: Madame de Tencin's (1682–1749) salon. Claudine Alexandrine Guérin de Tencin had a colourful and scandalous life. She was the mother of D'Alembert, *philosophe* and contributor to the *Encyclopédie*, whom she left on the steps of the *Saint-Jean-le-Rond de Paris* church a few days after his birth. From the 1720s to the 1740s her literary salon attracted leading intellectuals including Fontenelle, Montesquieu, Castel de Saint-Pierre, Marivaux, Alexis Piron and others.

94. **Temple de Gnide** (1725): prose poem in seven cantos by Montesquieu (1689–1755) arguing that true happiness comes from the heart rather than the senses.
95. **Abbé Pellegrin**: Simon-Joseph Pellegrin (1663–1745). French poet, playwright and librettist who collaborated with Jean-Philippe Rameau and other composers. See note 62.
96. **Bayle, Pierre** (1647–1706): French philosopher and writer best known for his seminal *Dictionnaire historique et critique* (1695–1697).
97. **Le Clerc, Jean**: also Johannes Clericus (1657–1736), Swiss theologian and biblical scholar famous for promoting exegesis, or critical interpretation of the Bible. Le Clerc parted with Calvinism over his interpretations and left Geneva for that reason. Among his other literary activities, he edited the *Bibliothèque universelle et historique* (Amsterdam: 25 vols, 1686–1693).
98. ***Espion turc***: or *Letters Writ by a Turkish Spy* (1687) by Giovanni Paolo Marana (1642–1693) is an eight-volume collection of fictional letters (published in 1683) claiming to have been written at the court of Louis XIV by an Ottoman spy named Mahmut.
99. **Lettres juives**: in English, *The Jewish Spy* (1765). Epistolary novel by the marquis d'Argens, published between 1738 and 1742. Purporting to be a translation of the correspondence between five distinguished rabbis who reside in different cities, the book comprises a discussion of the various governments of Europe.
100. **Procope**: in rue de l'Ancienne Comédie (6th arrondissement), it is reputed to be the oldest Parisian restaurant in continuous operation. It opened in 1686. Throughout the eighteenth century, the *Café Procope* was the meeting place of both the intellectual establishment and the literary scandalmongers.
101. **Servite Friars**: the Servite Order is one of the five original mendicant orders. The members of the Order use O.S.M. (for *Ordo Servorum Beatae Mariae Virginis*) as their post-nominal letters. The male members are known as Servite Friars or Servants of Mary. See note 103 below.
102. **Secularize**: to lift the monastic restrictions from a member of the clergy.
103. **Mendicant orders**: religious orders which depend directly on charity for their livelihood. In the Middle Ages, the original mendicant orders of friars were the Franciscans, the Dominicans, the Carmelites, the Servites, and the Augustinians.
104. **Foire Saint-Germain**: name given to the largely outdoor theatre put on at the annual fairs at Saint-Germain-des-Prés, featuring puppet shows and tightrope walkers, as well as legitimate comic plays.
105. **Snuffer**: functionary responsible for snuffing out the candles at the beginning of a play.
106. **Apollo's disciples**: poets and musicians. In Greek mythology Apollo (Ἀπόλλων), represented as a beardless, athletic youth, is recognized as a god of light and the sun, truth and prophecy, healing, music, poetry, and more.
107. **Merry-Andrew** (in French *Paillasse*, from the Italian *Pagliacci*): clown originally associated with a specific act at Bartholomew Fair. A person who clowns publicly: a buffoon.
108. **Messalina** (*c.* AD 17/20–48): third wife of the Roman Emperor Claudius. She was also a cousin of the Emperor Nero, second cousin of the Emperor Caligula, and great-great niece of the Emperor Augustus. A powerful and influential woman, she had a reputation for promiscuity.
109. **Marivaux**: French playwright (1688–1763). Pierre de Marivaux's most important works are *Le Triomphe de l'amour*, *Le Jeu de l'amour et du hasard* and *Les Fausses Confidences*. He also published a number of essays and two important but unfinished novels, *La Vie de Marianne* (1731–1745) and *Le Paysan parvenu* (1734–1735).
110. **Chyle**: from the Greek word χυλός chylos, 'juice'. Milky bodily fluid consisting of lymph and emulsified fats, or free fatty acids, formed in the small intestine. Monbron appears to use the word to signify a healthy physical constitution resulting from an active sex life.

111. **Plato** (Greek: Πλάτων): classical Greek philosopher (428/427 or 424/423 BC–348/347 BC), as well as mathematician, and a central figure in Western philosophy. The allusion here is to so-called platonic or non-sexual love.
112. **Origen** (Ωριγένης AD 184/185–253/254): scholar and early Christian theologian born in Alexandria. Eusebius reported that Origen, following Matthew 19:12, literally castrated himself.
113. **Pierre Abelard** (1079–1142): French scholastic philosopher, theologian and logician, famous for having been castrated as a result of his love affair with Eloise.
114. **Bits ... Pope**: testicles. An apocryphal tradition states that popes throughout the medieval period were required to sit on a special chair with a hole in the seat. A cardinal would then have the task of putting his hand up the hole to check whether the pope had testicles (in order to ensure he was not a woman in disguise).
115. **Salpêtrière**: originally a gunpowder factory (saltpetre is a constituent of gunpowder), converted in the seventeenth century to a hospital for the poor. La Salpêtrière served as a prison for prostitutes and a repository for the mentally disabled, criminally insane, epileptics, and the poor.
116. **Pathelin**: *La Farce de Maître Pierre Pathelin* (1457), best known of all medieval farces. Pathelin is a bogus lawyer in straitened circumstances who succeeds by flattery in getting a miserly draper to give him some cloth on credit. He later avoids payment by pretending he is mad. When asked by a shepherd to defend him at his trial, Pathelin's advice is that he should say 'baa' in answer to all questions. At the trial, the shepherd's accuser is none other than the draper. Seeing Pathelin, he repeatedly confuses the two crimes of which he has been the victim. His confusion, and the shepherd's 'baas', cause the judge to dismiss the case. Pathelin, however, when asking the shepherd for payment, only gets 'baa' in answer. It is a case of 'it takes a thief to catch a thief'. The quotation given here is not attributable to *Pathelin*.
117. **d'Argens**: Jean-Baptiste de Boyer, marquis d'Argens (1704–1771). French writer who fled France and settled at the Prussian court in the 1740s and 1750s. His subversive books were frequently denounced. These included *Lettres juives* (1738–1742), *Lettres chinoises* (1739–1742), and *Lettres cabalistiques* (1769); also the *Mémoires secrets de la république des lettres* (1743–1748), afterwards revised and augmented as *Histoire de l'esprit humain* (1765–1768). In addition to this he wrote six novels, the best known of which is *Thérèse Philosophe* (1748).
118. **Chevalier de Mouhy**: Charles de Fieux (1701–1784). One-time friend of Voltaire and prolific author of popular and mildly scandalous potboilers, including *La Mouche* (1736), *Le Masque de fer* (1737), and *Lamedis* (1735–1737). The last of these contains proto-Romantic metamorphoses, dream sequences and voyages to subterranean worlds.

SELECTED BIBLIOGRAPHY

Modern editions (by order of date published):

Margot la ravaudeuse, postface de Maurice Saillet (n.p.: Cercle précieux du livre, 1958); reissued (Paris: Jean-Jacques Pauvert, 1958, 1965)

The Amorous Adventures of Margot and *The Scarlet Sofa*, translated by Mark Alexander and L. E. LaBan [Lauraine Kirby], introduction by Hilary E. Holt (North Hollywood: Brandon House, 1967)

Margot la ravaudeuse, suivi de *Fanny Hill* de J. Cleland (n.p.: Cercle européen du livre, coll. 'Chefs d'œuvre interdits', 1972)

Margot la ravaudeuse, préface de Michel Delon (Toulouse: Zulma, 1992)

Margot la ravaudeuse dans *Romans libertins du* XVIIIe siècle, textes établis et présentés par R. Trousson (Paris: R. Laffont, 1993)

Margot la ravaudeuse, in *Romanciers libertins du* XVIIIe siècle, ed. by Patrick Wald Lasowski, tome I (Paris: Bibliothèque de la Pléiade, Gallimard, 2000)

Margot la ravaudeuse, *Le Canapé couleur de feu*, edited by Catriona Seth (Paris: *Le Monde* et Classiques Garnier, 2010)

Studies

BERKOV, P. N., 'Fougeret de Monbron et A. P. Sumarokov', *Revue des études slaves*, XXXVII, 1–4 (1960), pp. 29–38

BROOME, J. H., 'Voltaire and Fougeret de Monbron: A *Candide* Problem Reconsidered', *Modern Language Review*, LV (1960), pp. 509–18

——, 'Byron et Fougeret de Monbron', *Revue de Littérature comparée*, XXXIV (1960), pp. 337–53

——, 'L'Homme au cœur velu: the turbulent career of Fougeret de Monbron', *SVEC*, 23 (1963), pp. 179–213

BOUSSUGE, EMMANUEL, 'Fougeret de Monbron à la Bastille et dans ses archives', *RHLF*, 106 (2006), pp. 157–66

——, 'Enquête sur la réception de *Candide*', *Cahiers Voltaire*, 7 (2008), pp. 147–52

——, *Situations de Fougeret de Monbron (1706–1760)* (Paris: Champion, 2010)

LANGILLE, É. M., 'Molly, Jenny and Margot, or the Making of *Candide*'s Paquette', *Romance Notes*, 49 (2010), pp. 357–66

——, 'La Place, Monbron and the Origins of Candide', *French Studies*, 66 (1) (2012), pp. 12–25

——, 'La Place, Monbron et la Genèse de *Candide*', in *Les 250 ans de* Candide, ed. by N. Cronk and N. Ferrand (Louvain, Paris, Walpole MA: Peeters, 2014), pp. 337–46

PIZZORUSSO, ARNALDO, 'Situations and Environment in *Margot la ravaudeuse*', *Yale French Studies*, 40, *Literature and Society: Eighteenth Century* (1968), pp. 142–55

VENTURI, FRANCO, *Europe des Lumières: recherches sur le dix-huitième siècle* (Paris, La Haye: Mouton, 1971)

MHRA New Translations

The guiding principle of this series is to publish new translations into English of important works that have been hitherto imperfectly translated or that are entirely untranslated. The work to be translated or re-translated should be aesthetically or intellectually important. The proposal should cover such issues as copyright and, where relevant, an account of the faults of the previous translation/s; it should be accompanied by independent statements from two experts in the field attesting to the significance of the original work (in cases where this is not obvious) and to the desirability of a new or renewed translation.

Translations should be accompanied by a fairly substantial introduction and other, briefer, apparatus: a note on the translation; a select bibliography; a chronology of the author's life and works; and notes to the text.

Titles will be selected by members of the Editorial Board and edited by leading academics.

Alison Finch
General Editor

Editorial Board

Lightning Source UK Ltd.
Milton Keynes UK
UKOW06f0754030915

257968UK00001B/2/P

AMAZING WOMEN

Volume 1

DR CHARLES MARGERISON

The Amazing People Club®

Amazing Women

Published by Viewpoint Resources Ltd
Trading as Amazing People Club©

Viewpoint Resources Ltd
10 Grange Road, West Kirby, Wirral, Merseyside, England C48 4HA
Tel: +44 (0) 151 625 2332
Fax: +44 (0) 151 625 9961
Web: www.amazingpeopleclub.com

Represented by Amazing People Club LLC in North America

A BioView® story is a scripted virtual interview based on research about a person's life and times. As in any story, the words indicate only an interpretation of what the individuals mentioned in the BioViews® could have said. While the interpretations are based on available research, they do not purport to represent the actual views of the people mentioned. The interpretations are made in good faith, recognizing that other interpretations could be made. The inverted commas used in the BioViews® give an indication of possible dialogue in the context of the story. The author and publisher disclaim any responsibility from action that readers take on the BioViews® for educational or other purposes. Any use of the BioView® materials is the responsibility of the reader and should be supported by their independent research.

We recognise there are different conventions about the spelling of words in what we shall call British English and American English. We have chosen to adopt the British version, except for titles that focus on American individuals, where American English has been adopted.

ISBN: 978-1-921629-94-5

Design by Varjak Design www.varjak.com.au